DIPPER
OF
COPPER
CREEK

Jean Craighead George
and John George

Illustrated by Jean Craighead George

PUFFIN BOOKS

PUFFIN BOOKS
Published by the Penguin Group
Penguin Books USA Inc., 375 Hudson Street, New York, New York 10014, U.S.A.
Penguin Books Ltd, 27 Wrights Lane, London W8 5TZ, England
Penguin Books Australia Ltd, Ringwood, Victoria, Australia
Penguin Books Canada Ltd, 10 Alcorn Avenue, Toronto, Ontario, Canada M4V 3B2
Penguin Books (N.Z.) Ltd, 182-190 Wairau Road, Auckland 10, New Zealand

Penguin Books Ltd, Registered Offices: Harmondsworth, Middlesex, England

First published in the United States of America
in 1956 by E.P. Dutton & Co., Inc., a division
of Penguin Books USA Inc.
Published in Puffin Books, 1996

7 9 10 8

LIBRARY OF CONGRESS CATALOGING-IN-PUBLICATION DATA
to come

Printed in the United States of America

TO
CAROLYN J. CRAIGHEAD,
*who, with dignity and humor, shared her home
with foxes, eagles, owls, hawks, and people, and who,
by reshaping her adventures into unforgettable tales,
instilled the love of storytelling in all the
naturalists around her*

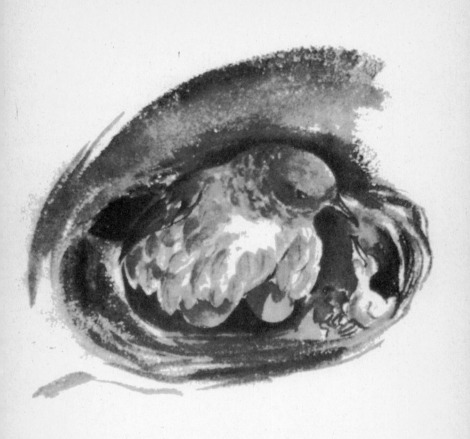

DIPPER OF COPPER CREEK

A brilliant flash of lightning was followed by an immediate explosion of thunder. Startled, Doug looked up at Gothic.

The lightning hit a tall spruce standing on the rimrock. The whole mountain shuddered and groaned.

Doug looked in horror and fascination as he saw the side of the mountain tremble and bulge forward. The cliff bellied and seemed to hang in space; each rock in its place.

Then the mountain fell! Millions of boulders flew out into space, broke into stones and hurtled down the mountain. The

noise was so loud, Doug heard it with pain; then he could not hear at all.

He was terrified. He could not run. Instead he calmly stooped down and picked up the tiny water ouzel. He came to his wits, turned, and ran.

"Much of the writing is sheer poetry while conveying accurate nature lore."
　　　　　　　　　　　　　　　—Christian Science Monitor

DIPPER OF COPPER CREEK

ACKNOWLEDGMENTS

A story of a region or a given species cannot be written today without using the vast fund of information gathered by many scientists over the years. To them we gratefully acknowledge our debt.

This story of the water ouzel, which is pronounced *oozel*, was written at the Rocky Mountain Biological Laboratory at Gothic, Colorado. Many scientists doing research there generously shared with us their findings and insight into the subalpine zone.

Finally, there is the ouzel itself. No one can know this bird without marveling at its extraordinary adaptation to a life in the swift streams of the high country.

CONTENTS

DIPPER OF COPPER CREEK

GOLD

RAIN clouds hung gray-blue and low over the ghost town of Gothic, lying two miles high in the Colorado Rockies. With no more sound than the flight of an owl, they swept over the sunblackened cabins and loosed their burden, drenching the townsite. Although it was the end of May, the glacial valley was a bowl of snow sitting high in the second range of the Elk Mountains.

Two thousand feet below in the town of Crested Butte it was spring. The snow was gone, the flowers were nodding along the roadways. Even the mountain peaks, that stood thirteen and fourteen thousand feet high, were snowless. At those skyscraping heights the alpine sun was like a torch that burned the ice away. Nevertheless, the peaks were cold, and the icy air that surrounded them poured into the valley and held the snow there until early June.

The month of May in Gothic town would have

looked like Christmas were it not for the tumbling pil-
lows of rain clouds that were bringing the thaw to the
valley of the high country.

Whispering Bill Smith was the only living man in
the snow-bound ghost town. The old prospector had
wintered in to run his trap line and for eight long
months he had listened to no voices other than those
of the trumpeting winds and the hardy Canada jays.

When the rainstorm had rolled on down the mountain, Whispering Bill slipped into his parka, picked up
his ax and walked out to his woodpile. He cracked
open a log with one swing, then leaned into the wind
and listened for a voice from the valley—the voice of
the sno-go that would soon leave Crested Butte and
open the road to Gothic.

The rotary snowplow was to bring young Doug,
Whispering Bill's teen-age grandson, into the high
country for the summer. He was a strong boy and
could help him carry down the ore from his mining
claims, located high in the mountain peaks above
town.

Whispering Bill was the only man alive who still
carried on the work of the old ghost town. After the
Civil War, when the price of silver was high, Gothic
had flourished—a busy, wealthy mining town of two
thousand people—people who had boasted of the visit
of President Ulysses S. Grant. But when the govern-
ment dropped the support of silver and went on the

gold standard, western towns like Gothic, Tincup, and
Leadville boarded their doors and windows. With the
crash of the silver market and the exhaustion of high
grade ore, the people could no longer make a living.
They moved away, leaving their homes to the wolves
and the grizzly bears. Now the aspens covered the rem-
nants of the old cabins, and as each year passed another
building fell beneath the pressure of the crushing snow.
In all of the old townsite only a half a dozen buildings
remained standing.

Whispering Bill was chopping the beams from old
Jim Juddson's cabin, which had finally succumbed to
the snows last March. As he chopped he thought about
Jim, who had died a rich man only a few years ago.
When he thought about Jim he always growled at himself for not having followed the old man up Rustler's
Gulch to his hidden lode; for Bill knew it was a rich
one. He couldn't say for sure how rich, but he knew
that Jim took only nine or ten bags of ore down in a
year, and still he lived in luxury in Pueblo during the
winter.

At times, the thought of that lode made Bill so restless that he had to stop whatever he happened to be
doing and go to look at the shining peak of Mt. Avery,
where he suspected that the lode lay hidden.

"Jim Juddson's lode!" he whispered hoarsely now, as
he swung around to face the glistening peak of Mt.
Avery. "He probably rolled a big boulder into that

sparkling little hole, so I couldn't find it. That would be his kind of joke. I can hear him sitting on that mountain now, laughing and laughing."

Whispering Bill shook his fist at the mountain.

"You told everybody where it was, Jim Juddson, and you told everybody different. That map you drew for me the week before you died! Why, that would be the last place in the world I'd look. That was a crazier map than the one I drew for you to my uranium strike up Dead Man's Gulch; but you went looking for it and were lost for three days! Those were the funniest three days of my life."

Whispering Bill had to sit down, he was so convulsed with laughter at the memory of Jim Juddson's futile search. The wind died down for a moment and he stopped laughing to stand up and look toward the pass. He thought he had heard the whirr of the snowplow. But the pass was motionless and as white as winter.

Bill's face was not just lined, it was creased like a crumpled paper bag. Long ago the smoothness had been worn away by the intense alpine sun and desiccating winds. Many hundreds of lines were now carved in his face. Even Bill's eyes were weathered by the high country. The whites were red, the once brown iris, milky; only the black pupils peered bright and clear into the snowflung dome of the Rockies. The man's voice had weathered, too. It was hoarse and sometimes barely audible. He was a short man, about five feet six, but stocky and hard. His sixty years showed only in the erosion of his face and hands.

The snowplow was not coming. Whispering Bill picked up his wood and went into his cabin. As he turned the doorknob he stopped and cocked his head. He smiled pleasantly. He heard beneath frozen Copper Creek the first muffled gurgle of the spring thaw. The water from the melting peaks was eating its way downstream. He heard the rain join the mountain water somewhere behind his grove of Englemann spruce, and before his eyes, the piling torrent cut open the stream bed. The long-silent creek was suddenly bubbling and singing beside his cabin.

"Gnad, gnad, gnad, chee chee chee, beeer!" a gray and black bird called from one of the spruce trees. Whisky, the Canada jay, who had spent the lonely winter with Bill, flicked his long tail and flew down to the woodpile.

Whispering Bill chucked his load of wood into the woodbox beside the stove and picked up a sourdough pancake that was left from his breakfast. He pitched it through the door to the bird. Whisky picked it up in his bill, winged off, dropped it and caught it with his feet. He carried it back to the spruce grove and devoured it with loud squawking noises.

Bill shut his door slowly, looking at Mt. Avery in the closing frame. His fortune lay there, and he liked to keep his eye on it from time to time during the day. Bill didn't trust the mountain. It might fall and plunge his latest claim into some obscure cirque. Furthermore he was sure the ghost of old Jim Juddson was sitting up there, waiting to blow the mountain top off if Bill discovered his lode.

"He'd do it if he could," he told the stove as he filled it with wood. The stove was old, but still handsome, with its shining brass curlie-wurlies as bright as the day they had been forged. "She looks pretty, and she burns pretty," Bill said of his antique. In a few minutes the teakettle that sat upon it hummed and boiled.

In the winter the stove had been the only source of heat. The cabin was insulated with gingham, paste and old newspapers that dated back sixty years. All together they had kept Bill quite comfortable in temperatures of fifty below zero.

In the far corner of the cabin was the bed, piled high with down comforters, and above it a shelf on which his boots stood. A table covered with worn oilcloth, a rocking chair, and two dynamite boxes for dining chairs, made up the rest of the furniture. A shelf of ore decorated the north wall, the south wall was shelved and stacked with supplies. A ladder staircase led to a low attic where a single bed, also piled with comforters, was ready for Doug.

Whispering Bill had turned his back to the stove to warm the seat of his pants when he heard the Canada

jay at the window. The bird was scolding for more food. The people of the high country call the Canada jay, "whisky-jack" or "camp robber," and so Bill called this fellow who came to fill his lonely hours, "Mister Whisky." His mate, "Mrs. Whisky," was shy and never came closer than the spruce grove.

Bill took a piece of toast from the breadbox and opened the door. The wind plastered his clothes to his body as he threw the toast into the snow and shouted, "Go on, Whisky, you old camp robber, you! Rustle up your own grub."

The bird flicked his wings together and soared toward the food. He broke his descent with a forward scoop of his wings and alighted on the bread. He carried it, as always, into the spruce tree and broke off large morsels with his beak. As he did, other pieces shattered to the ground, but he was too intent upon devouring what he had to notice the loss.

Mister Whisky was a versatile and intelligent bird. He enjoyed the proximity of people, more for their generosity than their company. He was an opportunist and sought out prospectors, campers and fishermen for a free handout. If he amused them for their kindness, it was incidental and not necessarily part of the bargain. He had one bird in mind—Mister Whisky. He was a rumpled-looking bird, his feathers bent and twisted. They never lay smoothly against his body, for they were dense and loose—insulation against the below zero weather. His head was white, but for a black band behind his eyes, which lent authenticity to his nickname "camp robber."

Whisky gulped the toast and was about to seek out his "resting" limb where he just sat after a heavy meal, when he saw a deer mouse gingerly crossing the snow beneath his eating tree. It was sniffing its way towards the fallen bits of toast. Whisky was stuffed, but he did not want anything else to eat his food, and he dived at the mouse to frighten it away. The mouse ran into the aspen thicket and Whisky jumped onto one of the larger pieces of bread. He carried it up Copper Creek to his resting perch and stood with it in his bill. He did not want to swallow it, so he poked it in a crotch a few steps up the limb. He fluffed his feathers, settled his feet and relaxed. The thought of the nearby food, however, worried him. Something might find it. He sidled to the crotch, pecked out the bread and swallowed it. It stuck in his throat, and he shifted his head three or four times before the food worked far enough down for him to be comfortable.

Feeling that a drink might help him, he nibbled at a patch of snow wedged between the limb and the branch of the tree. This was not enough. He flew to the edge of Copper Creek. He hopped to a shallow puddle and drank until the bread slid on down. Now he had the curiosity to cock his head and look at the material upon which he stood. It was a big dark slab of Niobrara limestone, the first bare rock of spring. Whisky ran all around it as if it were a long lost friend whose shape he had forgotten. He found a shallow water-filled pothole and waded in to take a bath.

Long, long ago the limestone had been deposited in a warm salty sea where the first birds swam in pursuit of fish; now, millions of years later, the Canada jay took a bath in it, thousands of feet above the level of the ocean where it began.

After bathing, Whisky preened beside his bath hole until his feathers were loose and dry.

There was a thundering roar up the stream from him, as an ice jam gave way at the cascades. Chunks of ice and tons of water roared down the narrow stream bed. Whisky leaped to his wings and flapped into a spruce just before the deluge swept over his rock.

"Gnad! beeeer!" he screamed at the exploding creek.

Into the tumbling, roaring waterway came a small gray bird, the color and the sleekness of the Niobrara limestone. He skimmed the grinding ice floes and flew through the bursting sprays as if the stream had created him, and were reluctant to release him to the sky. The bird alighted on the rock that Whisky had just deserted. He ran up and down the stone with the rise and fall of the stream, dipping and dipping and dipping at the end of each run.

Then he went back where he seemed to have sprung from, the lashing white waters of the opening creek.

Whisky cocked his head. The bird was gone. A block of ice rumbled over the spot where he had disappeared.

Up he came; bobbed in to shore on a swell, and stood on the limestone rock, dry and tidy. The wave that deposited the fragile bird swirled back into the stream bed.

Cinclus, the water ouzel, had arrived on his breeding grounds. He had followed the spring break-up from Crested Butte to the waterfall at the lower end of Gothic Valley. Here he had waited with other water ouzels, or dipper birds, for the thaw to open the cascades of the high country.

After the rainstorm Cinclus departed, flying over the snow-filled lower regions of the creek as swiftly as if a hawk were chasing him. As he passed Bill's cabin he heard the thunder that announced the release of Judd Falls and he came into the gorge just as the stream collapsed and opened.

Cinclus stood in the icy spray and dipped. He burst into song, as melodious and beautiful as the song of the mocking bird that might be heard in the deep southern regions of the continent. But the song of Cinclus was heard by none, for he sang to the accompaniment of the pounding waters of the mountains.

He sang effortlessly. Whisky, sitting ten feet away, heard one glorious note. The rest of the melody was drowned in a roaring gush of water that was carrying an enormous ice floe down the stream bed.

Across the narrow gorge a weasel slipped over a spruce root and grinned brightly at the water ouzel.

"Dek, ek, ek!" the alarm note of the dipper carried above the loudest din of the stream, and Whisky jumped to a higher limb, then checked to see what enemy was abroad.

He saw the long-tailed weasel ripple over the root and slide like a gold shadow along the water's edge. Whisky pushed off from his resting place and went banging through the grove, screaming as if his end had come. Other birds heard him and either took up the alarm or froze fearfully on their perches.

Cinclus had already flown to a rock in the cascades of Richard's Rapids. Here he was secure from any weasel and he went on with his singing, but the roar of the water was so thunderous that he could not even hear himself.

Whisky, having alerted the entire spruce grove, went back to find the weasel and give a step by step report of her doings. He thoroughly enjoyed the courageous assignment he had given himself.

"Gnad! gnad!" he pronounced at the foot of Richard's Rapids.

"Gnad!" he screamed at the edge of Bill's clearing.

"Gnad, gnad, gnad!" he screeched in desperation above the slushy yard.

Whispering Bill looked out his smudgy window to

see what mortal enemy Whisky was announcing. He
smiled as he saw the quick graceful weasel slip under
the woodpile. He called, "Well, Molly, where have you
been? I haven't seen you for two or three weeks. The
mice are eating my marten furs and I need you badly."
She heard him.

The weasel popped up between the logs on the top
of the woodpile. She smelled for him, but could not
locate him specifically. The entire cabin smelled like
him. She rippled down the logs, bouncing and gliding
until she could get under the footing of the cabin. It
was as if she had understood Bill.

Whispering Bill looked away from the weasel and
glanced down the valley. The eastern side of the gulch
had melted free of snow, but the western side was still
white. He rubbed the windowpane harder and peered
across the valley, for he thought he saw the snowplow
at the bend in the road. The window was still too dirty
for him to see clearly and he stepped to his door. He
shouted aloud as he saw a white geyser of snow shooting into the wind.

The plow pushed through the last deep drift and
moved slowly over the bridge that crossed Copper
Creek.

Young Doug jumped off the sno-go before it had
stopped. Leaping the slushy drifts he bolted toward the
cabin. Bill was overjoyed at the sight of the boy, but with

the characteristic reserve of the mountain man, said quietly, "Just kinda thought you might get through today."

Tom, who was running the big diesel plow, stopped the machine and climbed down. He walked over to shake Bill's hand and said, "I've got some supplies for you. John sent them up from the store. He said to tell you your horse is down in the flats below the last drift fence."

Bill nodded. Tom continued.

"The ranger is coming up in a day or so and he said he'd bring him up for you."

Bill nodded once more, then turned away from Tom to look at the grandson who was to be his summer companion. The boy was one of six grandsons and it was not until this minute that he was sure which one Doug was. The boy's father had been killed in an accident in the coal mines. That had been two years before the anthracite mines in Crested Butte closed down and left it another Colorado ghost town.

As the grandsons finished high school they went to work in Gunnison to help their mother support the younger children. Doug was one of the younger members of the family. Bill was not sure where he stood in the family line-up, but he was sure he was a fine lad. After all, he wanted to mine ore.

Doug was of medium height, broad and stocky like Bill. He had heavy brown hair, a well-defined chin, and good big features that already had a bony masculine

quality. Bill was a little disturbed by the honesty of the face, for a good prospector could not be telling all he knew; but he felt a summer under his tutelage would take care of that.

Bill concluded with some pleasure that Doug did not look unlike himself, and was pleased to see the Smith strain so strong. He was about to tell Tom about it when he saw that the plow driver was already seated in the cab, gunning the machine. Bill watched him edge on up through Gothic. Just beyond the black walls of Lee's Tavern, Tom turned the machine in a wide arc and started back.

Doug was standing beside Bill now, watching the plow move along the deserted main street of Gothic heading toward the bridge at Copper Creek.

When the plow was out of sight, Doug leaned down and picked the supplies out of the wet snow. He carried them into the cabin and placed them on the table. Bill followed him in, stirred the stove for the sixth time that day and added fuel. He turned and faced his grandson. The boy spoke first.

"Well, Grandpa, which crazy story about you is the real one?"

"None of them," Bill whispered. "I'm an old prospector, and I tell everyone I meet a different story."

"Are you really rich, Grandpa?"

Bill laughed aloud, and felt so good he reached for the sourdough starter and poured a bit into a bowl.

"Rich?" he asked, as he threw sugar, salt, and baking soda into the bubbly white mass. He chuckled while he beat down the rising thick batter. "Rich? Wait till you see what I have on Mt. Avery."

He picked up the bowl and flung open the door with his knee. The spoon in the batter thumped with a fine deep note. Whispering Bill thrust his chin toward the towering peak of Mt. Avery.

"Up there," he said, "where the wind screams and the rocks roar."

Doug looked from the mountain to the man, then stared at a bright pendant that hung on a gold chain around his neck. The pendant was a ground stone splotched generously with ore.

"What's that, Grandpa?" Doug asked. Whispering Bill closed the door with his heel, placed a skillet on the stove and dropped the first two pancakes into it. He spoke in a quiet, weather-beaten voice.

"Gold, boy. That's gold."

CINCLUS

CINCLUS stood on the rock in the middle of Richard's Rapids and listened to Whisky reporting the whereabouts of Molly, the long-tailed weasel. When the jay called somewhere near the prospector's cabin, Cinclus lost interest and boated out on an eddy behind the rock. He went down into the icy dark water to feed on the spring crustaceans that were hiding between the rocks and stones.

Cinclus was an extraordinary bird, no other passerine, or, for that matter, no other bird could live as he did in the breath-taking waterfalls of the alpine streams.

His slate-gray body was squat and compact, looking much like a worn glacial stone. Everything about him was designed for his life in the pounding waters. His tail was stubby and square; it would not hinder him in the fast-moving currents. His rounded wings were short, and the breast muscles that pulled them were large and strong. He could use his wings for flying, rowing, and maneuvering under water.

His plumage was also miraculous. It was fluffy and loose; yet he could plunge into the white foaming water and come up absolutely dry. His long, strong legs gave him the appearance of a shore bird, and they enabled him to wade into the shallow edges of the streams. His elongated toes ended in sharp, curved claws that held him to the rocks and stones beneath the rushing waters. They did not appear to be too different from the toes and claws of many other perching birds, still they held him to the rock surfaces in the swift waters.

His bill was shaped like an awl and with it he could pry into crevices in the rocks and under stones and boulders as he searched for food. Each long, linear nostril was covered with a small scale that capped off the water when he went into the pools and cascades.

Cinclus came up from the bottom of the ice-filled stream and floated down on the current. Just before the water plunged over the falls, he stepped lightly up on the big rock, dipped and sang.

The water ouzel would have been as inconspicuous as a shadow were it not for his flashing white eyelid. It was covered with a short, dense mat of pearly white feathers, and every time he blinked, which was almost as frequently as he dipped, his eyelid made a white flash. The dipping and the flashing made the bird stand out against the stones and the water.

In the Andes, in the Alps, in the Cascades, in the Himalayas, in the Rockies—wherever the white foam of the pounding mountain streams spills down into the valleys—there the dippers are at home. No other bird crowds them, for nature has evolved only the dippers to fill these niches of lonely wilderness beauty.

Cinclus stopped his song, for he saw another bird dipping in counter-movement to the downward flow of Copper Creek. He winged from his rock to investigate. The male ouzel of Judd Falls was arriving at his summer nesting territory.

Cinclus challenged him with a defiant "dek, ek, ek-ek," but did not chase him, for Cinclus was a first-year male and had no claim to the waters he was in.

The male of Judd Falls skimmed over his head, banked around the larger jutting outcrops and went up to the thunderous waterfall that dropped one hundred feet down the mountainside.

Judd Falls was part of the same geologic formation as Richard's Rapids. Millions of years ago when the earth buckled and heaved up the Rocky Mountains, a hard layer of diorite granite had been forced up through the softer limestones. The granite had resisted the cutting and digging of Copper Creek, while the limestones above and below the granite wore away. Judd Falls was the upper drop over the granite intrusion, and Richard's Rapids was the lower drop.

Cinclus watched the old, experienced male return to his territory and burst into song. Feeling that perhaps Richard's Rapids would be his own home, he flew from his rock and winged swiftly through the canyon to look at this land. He alighted on the shore opposite Bill's cabin and snapped up numerous cold insect larvae stirring numbly in the icy water.

The bird floated into the swift current, and used the surface action of the water to carry him across the stream. Any lesser creature would have been washed under the bridge in the time it took Cinclus to gain the far shore, but the bird understood each eddy and current, and used them to propel himself.

He ran up the shore, stopped and dipped by Whispering Bill's old water bucket, still frozen in the earth. He scooted around it, stopped and called his piercing, "De-ek," for smiling gleefully at him, her small white teeth clean and sharp between the furry lips, was Molly, the long-tailed weasel.

Cinclus was in the air, spinning toward the far shore by the time Molly had circled the bucket and lunged at him. She missed, but whipped and danced on the shore to tell the frightened ouzel that it was only fun, and to come back and play her devilish game.

Cinclus was back on his rock in Richard's Rapids by the time Molly was done with her dancing. Molly shifted to more promising prey.

In the dark shadows of the spruce grove, a sleepy

ground squirrel was resting at the entrance of his winter den, smelling the sweet odors of the dawn of the mountain spring.

He savored the last hours between sleep and the frantic three or four months of life that were before him. In this brief time he must raise young, bring them to independence, and harvest enough food from the mountain valley to make him fat and sleek for next winter's long hibernation.

His dry nose drew in the cold afternoon air, and he fluttered his hind legs as his blood warmed and slowly awakened him.

His ears were neat and mouselike, his tail not much bigger than a chipmunk's. In fact, he looked very much like a chunky chipmunk with a light, black-bordered stripe down the side of his golden-mantled fur, but he had no stripes on his face.

He pawed the snow at his den entrance and was about to pull himself to a pocket of rain water when he saw and scented Molly.

Molly was ranging toward him. The golden-mantled ground squirrel slid back into his tunnel, kicked up dirt and needles to block the entrance, and put off his spring debut. He pushed far down into his tunnel, then climbed to a high, dry pocket that was lined with last year's bedstraw weeds. Here he licked his cold feet, and slipped into a sleep lighter than his deep hibernation slumber.

Although it was late in May and only the western slope was free of snow, the spring of the high country was lying just beneath the cover. In the moist meadows where patches of snow had already vanished, the pointed green shoots of the mountain iris were standing in the sun.

More wonderful than the iris were the avalanche lilies. They arose and bloomed in the receding snow, and all through Gothic valley their gold heads bobbed against the ice. At night they closed their petals and withstood the freeze and the bitter winds that roared down from the peaks.

The buttercups were also above the ground in the slowly opening alpine meadows, and many of the hardy mountain grasses were coloring the mountain clearings yellow-green.

The brief, abundant plant life of the high Rockies had begun beneath the snow cover, for it must come to bloom and seed before the autumn of late August and the winter of mid-September. All the alpine life was racing against time. In the plant world, only the hardy perennial species survived the severity of the mountain sun, wind, and ice. The annuals of the lowlands could not mature their seeds in a season so short and they were eliminated at the foot of Gothic Valley.

As the days passed, more and more life stirred in the high country. Like the golden-mantled ground squirrel, the hibernating mammals awakened slowly. The whistling marmot was one of these.

The rock slide above Judd Falls faced the afternoon sun. The snow had melted from it and run into the creek almost a week ago. Still the marmot of that rock slide had come out on his desolate estate only once or twice for it was too early to forage in the almost life-less land. It was better to lie half-asleep and half-hungry in his warm burrow than to fight the biting winds and be starved. The few scant blades of grass that he could find would be scarcely enough fuel to keep him warm.

The slope in which the marmot slept was the wind-way for the howling draughts that rushed valleyward from the peaks of Red Mountain and White Mountain.

Marmota, the marmot, was not satisfied with his territory, but last fall there had been numerous young marmots searching for a piece of land. Many had lost their lives. Marmota had been pushed and chased from several other areas. Winter was close upon him, the mountain tops were snow-covered. He had been chased into the talus slope above Judd Falls, and was about to be run off that by a young male, when he turned and fought.

Marmota, the tired victor, dug his burrow while the first snow blew into the niches and cracks. He crawled into it in late September.

In mid-April something aroused him from his death-like sleep of hibernation. The temperature of the earth had not changed greatly and he could not see the wider arching of the sun, but his eyes were open, and he was coming to life like the seeds and the bulbs, deep in the earth. It was the breeding season for the marmots. After a week, the females returned to their burrows and Marmota retired to his rock slide to sleep until the meadows were green with grasses.

It was the need for water that finally brought him out for the summer. He walked ponderously down his passageway and pushed away the earthen plug he had put in his burrow. The blinding alpine sun forced him to close his eyes, and he lay in his burrow until he was accustomed to the light. The sun warmed him, and

presently he arose and remembered that he was desperately thirsty.

He walked slowly down the side of the mountain to
a brook that had its source in the melting ice field
above the slide. Marmota drank as if he would never
satisfy his thirst.

The sun, the water, and the exercise loosened his

muscles and he trotted back to his den with more spirit. Beside his doorway was a large rock. He stretched upon it and immediately slept. The sun burning through the high thin air warmed him to his belly.

Marmota was not so deeply asleep that his nose was not working. It twitched and twitched, then stopped; and Marmota was on his feet and in his burrow, before the scent of the coyote was more than a faint wisp.

Canis, the coyote, loped out of the spruce forest above the slide, and jogged down to the hole into which his prey had disappeared. His long dog-like nose sucked up the sweet scents of the marmot, and whetted his appetite for this large tasty rodent. Eager for this succulent game, he loped up to the talus slope looking for another marmot that might be a little drowsier than Marmota.

Cinclus, the water ouzel, on his flight up the canyon saw the gray, shaggy Canis trotting along the rimrock above him. He called, "De-ek," but without great feeling, for Canis was not a threat to the dipper. He was a predator, however, and deserved some recognition from a bird who was establishing his territory and waiting for a mate.

His "De-ek" was answered with a strong, loud authoritative "DE-EK," and a steely bird zoomed around the jutting spruce toward him. Cinclus fled before a storming male who had returned to his territory. Cinclus deeked and fought, but the male ouzel of

Richard's Rapids knew the territory too well. He chased Cinclus over the falls and into the Niobrara wall, before the younger bird remembered that it was there.

In the tussle Cinclus left a few breast feathers at Richard's Rapids, then took his leave.

He winged past the cabin where Whispering Bill was saddling his horse, Lodestone, for young Doug. He swooped under the bridge and down through the meadowland. Suddenly, as if he had an inspiration, he banked and turned up the crystal branch of Copper Creek that cut around the foot of Gothic Peak.

This fork was fed by the glacier that had cut the peaks at the head of the valley, Mt. Baldy and Mt. Belleview, while the other fork roared down from the glaciers and snowfields that hemmed Copper Lake, over which towered White Mountain and Mt. Avery.

Cinclus flew faster and faster, following the creek around the sharp bends and past black-widowed cabins. He heard the splashing of the rollicking runnels spilling down Gothic Mountain as the snow fields melted.

He only glanced at the bubbling cascades under him, for he was moving upstream, knowing with the instinct for water signs inherent in a dipper bird that a cascade was not far away.

As he passed the old assay house that stood at the top of the limestone canyon, a Townsend's solitaire

winged out for an insect and returned to the wall. Suddenly he heard the falls. He dashed around the last bend and dropped onto a smooth black boulder at the foot of the veil of water that was Vera Falls.

He dipped and dipped and dipped, sang, and plunged into the roiling foam of the falls. He rode to the bottom on a swirl, grasped a minute crack in a boulder with his toes and listened to the noisy floor of the stream. Rocks hitting rocks, stones being ground into sand, pools being dug, canyon walls being slowly undermined.

The sun penetrated into the depths of the stream, for the water was like glass. Cinclus poked around the rock until he found some small crustaceans to eat, then he pumped his wings and bounced to the surface.

Around and around he swam, cork-like, for he sat higher on the water than a duck. He let a forceful current sweep him downstream, turn him around and around and carry him under the far moss-covered bank. He ran ashore and pecked the pebbles as he hunted food.

That was enough of the bottom of the falls. He flew up the cascade, riding high enough to keep his breast above it, and low enough to flick his wings in the foam. He alighted on a great boulder that divided the waterfall into two parts. Before him was a narrow flume into which the entire stream was squeezed. It was leaping and roaring. Above it was another falls, a man-made dam, built by the silver miners of Gothic to course the water into their stamp mill. The dam had fared better than the mill, for where the mill had been there remained only an old rusted boiler and gooseberries and aspens.

Above the miners' dam, the stream spread out and rippled peacefully through an alpine meadow.

Cinclus dipped up and down in great excitement, then flew up the flume, over the dam, and into the meadow. He coasted to a rock bar and gathered many mouthfuls of the larvae of the caddis fly. The meadow stream abounded in this food so important to the diet of dippers.

A rustle in the willows startled him, and he flew across the stream. Odocoileus, the mule deer, was bringing her fawn of the season to the stream for the first time. Cinclus relaxed as he watched the young animal spread its front feet to sniff the water. Odocoileus was the most nervous of the three. She kept turning her big funnel-ears into the wind, and tasting the breezes to the right and left.

The fawn was very young. It had been born only a week before, and was still awkward and unskilled. Cinclus felt the youngness of it with some pleasure, for this was the beginning of the season for the babies of the wilderness, a most pleasant time in the high country where the young frolicked openly in their playgrounds far from the pressure of man.

The fawn saw the bird dipping on the sandbar. The movement fascinated him. The bird kept going up and down. A nudge from his mother brought the fawn to her heels and he followed her reluctantly into the willow grove. He looked back before he came to the dark spruce forest, and saw that the bird was still bouncing.

Cinclus spent the next few days singing on every rock and root of his waterway. His trilling song of the water and rocks was sung to Vera Falls. The falls outvoiced him with a booming roar.

Cinclus knew that other ears heard that song. A young male coming up the stream must have heard it for he flew high above the falls and disappeared into the upper waters of the stream.

No other male came to challenge Cinclus. Already he felt that this was his territory. He even relaxed at times and flew right into the falling water. He did not go down with it, but burst through into an airpocket behind the falls. Here he settled on a small ledge, looking out at the water-blurred forms that were the trees and mountains. At these moments he felt completely secure. No land enemy could track him, nor could the red-tailed hawk that combed the mountain meadows see him. He was beyond all doubt the safest bird alive, so well protected was he by the water for which he was so marvelously adapted.

On the third morning after his arrival at Vera Falls, Cinclus was feeding at the bottom of the roaring flume.

He watched for an upriding current, hopped into it and was shot to the top of the water. He floated in to shore with the current. There was another dipper sitting on an old beam at the dam.

Cinclus challenged, but this time the challenge led to no fight. Dip, dip, dip he went. He dropped his wings and fluttered them. The other bird watched but did not acknowledge the greeting. Teeter, a female, had arrived, but Cinclus was not yet sure that she was not another male. There were no bright colors or other markings to tell him.

Cinclus chased her into the meadowland and then for the first time he realized that this new bird was to be his mate. She did not fight back. Eagerly Cinclus led her along Straight Edge Pool, past Bar Rapids, around Beaver Pond to the quiet waters of Open Flat. Then he grounded and faced her, for this was the upper limit of his territory. There was another pair of dippers beyond.

Teeter stopped, for she understood the limits of their land. Cinclus poured out his flowing song, and Teeter listened. Cinclus was an extraordinarily beautiful singer, and Teeter dipped her acknowledgment.

When the song of the upper end of the territory was done, the two birds took their way downstream to the lower reaches of their land. They flew, swam, and hunted along the crystal stream, taking time to enjoy the runnels from Gothic Mountain, blue-shadowed and restless.

At the bridge where the branch of Copper Creek met the main body of water, they stopped and fed. Cinclus would not go beyond the invisible line that he and his neighbor had marked off before Teeter's arrival.

After feeding awhile, Teeter winged all the way back to Vera Falls without stopping. There she alighted on the jutting beam of the old dam and studied a dome of intricately woven moss fastened on the face of the canyon wall.

THE BOY WHO
CAME TO GOTHIC

THE trail to Bill's claim was still snowbound. The day after Doug arrived, Bill looked at the white peak of Avery and the snowy edges of the high meadows and judged that it would be two weeks before they could do any mining. The winter snowfall had been heavy. It would be June before the upper trails were open.

Two weeks was no time at all to Whispering Bill, for time rides swiftly for a man of sixty years, but to Doug two weeks was a long, long time. When Bill made this decision Doug gasped. His enthusiasm for the summer work exploded and almost was replaced by tears. He did not see how he could wait that long.

Doug was in his teens and everything within him needed action. He would run rather than walk. He broke dishes in his haste to be done with them. He never crawled into bed, he jumped. Now he felt that the decision of the old man was preposterous. What were a few snowdrifts? They could cut a path through them. If Grandpa couldn't, he could!

He was about to beg, when he saw that Whispering Bill was rocking quietly in his chair, reading the mining news. He looked as if he were settled for two weeks. Doug banged out of the cabin, slamming the door.

He strode down Copper Creek watching the rushing, bubbling mountain water that was more in keeping with his spirit.

He stopped when the stream became too treacherous to follow and looked about him. Gothic Mountain rose like a cathedral before him, its Gothic spires distinct in afternoon light.

There seemed to be no life for miles and miles around. With a sob of disappointment he threw himself on a sand-colored boulder and wished with all his strength that he were back in Crested Butte.

It had been a deep struggle for Doug to leave the Butte and come to the high country to dig ore with Grandpa. His mother had not wanted it, but he had finally convinced her to let him go, only to discover that he was unsure. He carried it through, however, and it was with a brave face that he rode up the long, lonely road to Gothic. The excitement of the first day

was proving it a wonderful idea; then suddenly, this
afternoon, everything burst. He was as unhappy now
as he had been happy a few hours before.

He thought of his mother. Last fall she had made
arrangements for him to deliver groceries during the
summer. Everything had been arranged until Grandpa
snowshoed into town for Christmas. He enlivened the
evenings with tales of gold strikes, silver veins, and
men who came down from the mountains and bought
whole towns.

Doug's mother had sighed as she listened to her

father, for she remembered other details, omitted from his stories. There had been the cold nights, the hungry weeks and months that went by, her mother taking in laundry to feed the family, and the bubble of a fortune that always burst just before Grandpa reached it.

Then she would remember that this was many years ago, and that Grandpa was a good storyteller. It was not unpleasant to see him sitting by the fire with her two younger boys, telling once again the tales of the high country.

One morning Doug came to his mother and threw his arms about her.

"Ma!" he said, "Grandpa is going to use me this summer. He has given me a job helping him in his mine."

For a moment Mrs. Kriserich could not believe her ears. What did her father have in mind, telling this youngster that he could give him a job? He could barely support himself.

"That's ridiculous," she said with finality. "Tell Grandpa you can't go. Everything is settled for you to work at John's store."

"That's no fun; that's just plain dull!" Doug had shouted. Mrs. Kriserich had stood back and looked at Doug curiously. He meant it. She spoke to Bill later when the boys were out.

"Pa, please," she said. "We suffered so, we hated the

ups and downs. You don't know the shame we faced with you never getting more than a few dollars here and there.

"You just can't take Doug up there prospecting. He's having enough trouble trying to settle down and find his place. I don't want him to be a good-for-nothing."

"Well, Peggy," Bill whispered with a twinkle in his eye. "Better a good-for-nothing, than a Mommy's boy. Eh?"

When Grandpa snowshoed off into the white wastes, he left the family in a dither, as usual. Doug was beginning to feel the need for independence and wider horizons, and Peggy was beginning to realize how much she did run her boys' lives. There was no social life in Crested Butte since the mines had closed, and the energy she had once put into the church and school socials was now directed into her home. She had turned the full force of her organizing ability on Doug, and she knew it.

For many months mother and son discussed and argued, until finally Peggy consented. After all she could not pass on to her son the miseries of her own childhood. He must go and find out for himself. Furthermore, spring was coming, and the ice fields would be melting. There would be avalanche lilies and purple iris blooming in the snow. The crystal cascades would open and splash down the mountains. When she thought of spring and summer in the high country, she almost forgot the sorrows.

She had managed to get a message up-country to Grandpa by way of the ranger who was going to the hills on patrol. For if she knew her father, now that he had stirred things up, he would already have forgotten the invitation he had so generously extended. She was not going to have Doug disappointed the moment he walked into the dreary cabin.

Whispering Bill got the message and was truly moved. Indeed he had forgotten the tempest he had stirred in Crested Butte, but the thought of having a grandson spend the summer with him made him happy. He had wished that he could remember which boy it was going to be.

The first night in the cabin, the old man and the boy spent a wonderful evening together. Bill told vivid stories of the mining camps, and Doug listened to this high adventure with all his heart. He was the perfect audience for the old fellow, and when they retired that night, both were matchlessly happy.

The following afternoon when Bill announced the two-week delay, the elusive bubble that his mother had so often described appeared and broke.

Doug returned from the rocks of Copper Creek an hour later, and found Grandpa sitting on the old timber that was the step to the cabin. He was doing nothing, and the sight of him forced Doug to whine, "Grandpa, what'll I do for two whole weeks?"

Whispering Bill shrugged his shoulders. He didn't believe in telling a young fellow how to spend his time. Loneliness would create something or the boy would not be worth his salt on the desolate trail.

A "gnad, cheese," sounded from the spruce limb above the woodpile, and Whisky banged out of the boughs to tell Bill that he was hungry.

Whispering Bill squinted at the jay and spoke real words to him.

"Whisky, where have you been? Showing off for your girl, eh? Well, you haven't been around all day, and I don't know as how I'm gonna feed you." Whereupon he got up, went into the cabin, and came back with a slice of bread generously spread with peanut butter.

Doug forgot everything but the sight of the bird coming closer and closer to his grandfather. It seemed as if the whisky-jack were answering him in hoarse jay utterances. He flew to the roof of the cabin, and from there he dropped onto the worn brown hand. Whisky twisted off a large bite, gulped it, and flew back to the spruce bough.

Doug asked for the bread with his outstretched hand. He was afraid to speak. Whispering Bill gave it gladly. Breathlessly Doug held it out to the camp robber. The bird studied him for a full minute with his

right eye and then alighted on his hand. It was a rare moment for Doug, and he did not breathe while Whisky gobbled, even though his sharp claws pricked his skin. He could see the tiny gray feathers around the bright black eye, and the dense ones of his breast. Here was something alive and friendly that had winged out of the enormous loneliness of this wilderness. Doug looked into the dark spruce forest and knew it was not empty.

Whispering Bill tipped his hand to Whisky and went into the cabin. Two weeks was no time at all in the high country. Doug would no sooner learn the habits and haunts of the jays than it would be time to take to the trail. He wondered if he should really open the wonders of the wilderness to the boy. The birds and animals could become more fascinating than the cold silent veins of rock.

Doug held the bread a long time before it came to him that Whisky was no longer eating, but was breaking off pieces and carrying them into the spruce grove. He listened. He was sure he had heard a second jay hiding in the drooping boughs. He walked softly across the spongy earth and parted the limbs. There on a high limb was Whisky with another bird. It looked exactly like him. They were whispering as they ate, and since Doug no longer knew which was Whisky and which was the strange bird, he sat down to figure it out. One jay was bowing and presenting the other with a piece of bread. The second jay, acting as coy as Mary Ann Bates when you asked her to dance, took the bread in her bill, then in her feet, and finally condescended to eat it.

When he realized one was Mr. Whisky and one was Mrs. Whisky, he dropped his head against a tree and thought about the birds and how pleased his mother would be to see them. It was quiet in the spruce grove and his thoughts wandered. He was back in Crested Butte again in the living room at home. His mother was standing before him saying:

"Son, Grandpa is a fine old man, but he has never found anything in those mountains. Just rocks, heartaches, and poverty." Doug repeated her words. Grandpa had postponed the trip, maybe because there wasn't anything on Mt. Avery. His mother could be right. Then Doug had an idea of his own. Maybe Grandpa didn't really care about gold and silver at all. Maybe he was up here alone because he loved the high country.

Whisky flicked Doug with his wing and alighted on a low branch of the tree. Doug jumped and before he realized what he was doing, he spoke to the bird.

"Whisky, whatever is the matter?" The bird answered with a soft call, so unlike his rowdy pronouncements, that Doug wondered if Mrs. Whisky could have laid an egg.

Actually he was calling his mate. She was not too

far away brooding their newly hatched young.

The idea that the jays might have an egg brought Doug to his feet and he decided to follow Whisky and see.

The bird seemed to co-operate with this plan. Whisky flew a few feet then stopped and looked back to see if Doug was coming. Doug crashed after him in high excitement.

Whisky found this game a fine one, for he was leading Doug as fast as possible away from the nest. He was delighted that his trick was working so well. Hopping from rock to bough he took Doug to the most remote corner of his territory. It was a spot he was not too sure of himself, for another jay occasionally camped there, but it was a good place to leave the boy. It was right where the Gothic branch met Copper Creek.

Doug pushed through the willows to the water, then searched for Whisky. He was nowhere in sight, and there was no nest, not even a tree.

Doug laughed. He knew he had been tricked. It didn't matter, it was a good one on him. He sat down on a gray weathered boulder that was splattered with circles of red and yellow lichens, and tossed a pebble into the rushing water. He lifted his eyes and watched the dazzling white clouds sweep over the massive peak of Gothic Mountain.

All at once he realized how wonderful it was to be

on his own. He had walked half a mile or more without telling anyone where he was going. Nobody, but one crazy old jay, knew he was here. It was almost like being a man.

High up in the mountain he saw a gale start at timberline and sweep down into the meadowlands, springing the trees as it went. A few Audubon's warblers rode down with it. Doug could see their yellow throats and crowns as they found low perches in the protected trees along the stream.

Then the cold wind reached Doug and he shivered. He had really not put on enough clothing this morning. It had always been his mother who had thought of things like heavy jackets and extra socks. Grandpa had never said a word about what a person should and should not wear in the high country. For a moment he felt neglected.

Then he remembered the chore that Grandpa had assigned him. He was to put the cornmeal mush on the stove for an hour each evening to prepare for breakfast. He thought of home and the ease of having Mother do such tasks. Being a man on your own was full of conflicts, like wanting to live in the wilderness, but not being quite ready to do all the dull things that went with it. Doug arose and stretched for the sprint home.

A "zeet" rang from the stream bed, and Doug turned to see what had called. Had it been a call? The water rushed and sped over the stones and quietly pooled at his feet. Perhaps it was a trick of the water.

The boy rubbed his eyes and looked into the pool. He thought he had seen a bird under the water, a little bird that ought to be singing in a tree. He had heard that some people got "altitude fever" the first week or so in the high country. He wondered if he had it and if it made you see birds in the water; but then he saw it again. A bird in a cage of water, hopping around way down on the bottom, turning stones and jabbing at unseen things.

Doug started to drop to his knees. The bird apparently saw his awkward start, for it opened its wings and flew up through the water. There were a few circles where it took the air in its wings and abandoned the stream. Then it was acting like any little gray bird flying away from danger.

Doug ran after it; splashing through the shallow water, running past deep pools on the rocky bank. He ignored the voice that called from his childhood reminding him that he should not get wet.

He followed the bird deeper and deeper into the wilderness, now running, now wading, now climbing. From time to time he would lose it, and then he would round a bend and see it riding on the water like a duck, or running along the shore like a sandpiper.

He stopped in the canyon below the old assay house, for he heard ahead of him the thunder of a high falls

and he wondered if he could get out of the canyon at all.

Then he saw the bird dipping up and down on a rock in the middle of the rushing stream and he splashed on.

Cinclus was quite a different bird from Whisky. He neither feared nor sought man. The running boy did not alarm him, neither was he curious about him. He was just a boy running and splashing in the water, much like a young fawn. Cinclus knew the whisky-jacks and had observed them begging from campers and fishermen, but man was so unimportant to him that he neither liked him as the jays did, nor feared him as the deer did. He was not shy either, just self-sufficient. Whisky was an obvious bird, bold, loud, one of the first birds or animals a stranger saw upon coming into the high country. Cinclus was gray like the stones, part of the water. One discovered an ouzel only after becoming acclimated and sensitive to the country.

Cinclus had been hunting for an hour and was ready to rest. He flew up the runnel that dropped down the face of Gothic Mountain. He alighted on a favorite moss-covered rock. Beside it bounced an exquisite blossom of an alpine columbine, crisp and perfect. This was the very first columbine of the season, a flawless flower with snowy white petals, tipped with pale blue trumpet-like tubes.

Doug did not see the bird go up the runnel, and he walked past him. He rounded a bend, crawled over a

pile of logs and stood at the foot of Vera Falls. When he
saw it he knew he must climb it. The route that he
picked up the rocks was so close to the spray that it
beaded his face with droplets. He gained the top, and
looked up the narrow flume and saw the old dam.

Doug walked up to the last touch of man in this lost
country at the top of the Rockies. The sight of it made
him desperately lonely. The men who had made it
were so far away in cities, in towns, in graves. Suddenly he wanted to hear Grandpa's voice, or see a sign

of life. He looked across the flume at a dome of moss that could be a nest, some creature's "home" in this solitary canyon. It was an attractive nest, with an entrance at the bottom like an igloo. Doug tried to think what animal would build a home there, and as he thought of some little creature living there, he felt better.

It grew dark early and swiftly below the peaks, and Doug turned and ran homeward, for the stream bed was now in the shadow of the mountain.

In the cabin he found Bill splitting kindling. Doug saw the pot of mush on the stove. He waited a moment to receive his scolding, for he had forgotten his chore and was soaked to the skin. No scolding came. Although his teeth were now chattering, there was not even a suggestion that he change his wet clothes. Did this silence mean that Grandpa considered him old enough to take care of himself?

He shivered as he struggled out of his wet clothes. He thought of home; the warm fireplace, the good stew ready to dip and eat. He dressed by the stove, trying to think of some of the unhappy times at home. He could think of none until he stopped shaking. Once warmed, he remembered the hours of boredom that had been his in the deserted town.

Whispering Bill did not seem to notice the boy's thoughtful silence. He went about setting the table, and when he was finished he called pleasantly to Doug.

Doug pulled on another sweater and bounded to the dynamite box that was his seat.

While they ate canned hash, Doug told of the bird in the water. He described it with some disbelief in his own observations. Bill smiled and leaned over his bowl.

"You aren't crazy, boy, and don't think you've got the 'altitude,' 'cause what you saw was correct.

"That little fellow is called a water ouzel, or dipper bird, and its got more sense than any other bird in the world. It should have been called 'the prospectors' bird,' 'cause where that bird goes, so go old dogs like me.

"I've seen those little birds way up in the waterfalls of Mt. Avery. I've talked to them and told them where my silver is; and they don't rush down and get a lot of diggers up there, they just go on liking the water, and hunting bugs and raising young. They live in the prettiest places in the world, and they know it, and that's all they care about. Oh, they're great little birds."

Bill's voice wore down to a whisper, and now he was speaking of the ouzel that had nested almost on top of his richest find. Bill had been working hard the day he saw the bird, and stopped now and then to look at the dipper and consider its wisdom. The bird lived to enjoy the splashing water, the dark stunted trees of timberline, and the banks of alpine flowers that bloomed like a paint palette along the waterway.

That afternoon he had almost blacked-out from

working too hard at thirteen thousand feet after coming from the lowlands. He left his hole in the mountainside and fell toward the stream. He fought the dizzy darkness in his head. Then the dipper diving and plunging in the water caught his attention and he concentrated on the bird to keep himself awake. When he finally pulled out of the dizziness, he stopped mining for the day and walked through the rocky gorges with his fishing rod. The cascades and the flowers and the rocks had always looked different after that day.

Doug felt much better. He was warm and full of food, and his grandfather was speaking of something he knew. It was very cozy. It was also a triumph. He had found the bird that his grandfather admired the most.

Doug stretched out on Bill's bed to listen. His spine pressed into the down comforter and he was asleep.

Bill finished his journey into the past to himself.

He took the overdone mush from the stove and hung Doug's boots in a warm spot where they would dry by morning.

THE NEST ON THE CANYON WALL

TEETER, the mate of Cinclus, the water ouzel, alighted on the jutting beam of the mining dam and looked down the flume. In her bill was a stalk of dried grass. This piece of grass had been carefully selected. It was well cured, dry but not brittle, having aged slowly in the air and shade. The bird felt the rightness of this blade and she came to the old dam to dip and dance before she carried it to the nest on the canyon wall, the very nest that Doug had seen.

Lining the nest was not just a chore for Teeter. It was a ceremony and to do the job well required many little niceties on the part of both birds.

Teeter was dipping high on the dam, her white eyelid flashing. She tilted back her head and worked the strand of grass through her bill until she held it by the tip. Then from the bottom of the falls she heard the song of the ouzel. Cinclus had seen her standing high above the cascade with the first grass for the nest and he threw back his head and voiced his melody of the waterfall.

Teeter was reassured by the song and bowed to her songster. Then she flew down the flume to the wall of limestone. The precious stalk of grass trailed behind her. She alighted alongside the dome of moss that was her nest. The nest was a little wider than the ledge that supported it. The low door opened into space and flying spray.

Teeter had built this nest a year ago. She was a young bird then, and had never constructed a nest before. There had been an old male dipper who had courted her when she came winging up-mountain. He had sung and encouraged her as she worked and when she had finished, she had built a dipper nest, like all other dipper nests. Her instincts had guided her. The old male was her partner in the rituals of the ouzel birds, helping her where there were no instincts to direct her.

They raised one young ouzel who fledged from the nest above the rushing flume. After the nesting season they had all flown to the lowlands where they separated.

That winter, the old male, as if he had completed

his work, succumbed to one of the terrible winter nights of the Rockies.

It happened during a cold wave in January. For days it was difficult to get down through the ice and snow into the water, where the ouzels searched for the dormant insect eggs and larvae.

Late one afternoon the old male dipper had to break a thin film of ice to get back up through a plunge hole. At first he could only get his head and neck out. He pumped and pumped his wings until he finally wedged through the ice film. His feathers were wet and he was cold. He ran to a niche in the rocks, out of the path of the biting wind, where he could preen and remove the water. But darkness fell before he could dry his feathers, and he never grew warm again. The temperature dropped far below zero and the old male, who had helped young Teeter to become a mother of the wilderness, slept on and on.

When spring came Teeter left the wintering grounds of the ouzels and flew alone up Copper Creek. She did not know if the old male would meet her. She hurried, for she desired one thing—to get to Vera Falls. She did not stop to explore other falls as did the younger females. They did not know where they would spend the summer, and they checked all the possibilities. Teeter knew, and she wasted no time along the way.

Teeter traveled swiftly. A few days ahead of her

were the male dippers, who left the lowlands early to establish their nesting grounds.

Teeter was the first of the females to go into the mountains. Up the snowy glacial valleys she flew, always following the streams, flying low and clinking her soft notes. She did not sing like the males. She clinked, and her voice sounded like stones rolling and bumping under the water.

Teeter flew faster as she turned into the tributary of Copper Creek, and she stopped only once for food before she reached the lacy falls. She dipped in great excitement on the old rock below the cascade, recalling every toe-hold and angle of the stone.

She spread her gray wings and swooped up the falls to the giant boulder that split the water into a shawl of bubbles and spray.

There at the foot of the miners' dam was Cinclus. He was strong and large, and his gray feathers were pressed to his body with the smoothness of a mountain stone. She had passed no other dipper on the way upstream from Copper Creek bridge. As she came up the falls and looked at Cinclus, her entire attention was given to him. She studied his mannerisms and appearance, and in this way she learned he was a male, although he looked just like her.

As she looked at Cinclus she felt the nearness of her nest, the plentiful food of the thundering falls, and the potentialities of life within her body.

Then Cinclus sang. Some birds sing more beautifully than others, and although each species of bird has a song to sing, each individual does it a little differently.

Cinclus could sing the song of the dipper birds with more beauty and fullness than any other male in the Rockies. He had extraordinary control and richness, and ended his song with a note whose tone could not be matched by instrument or bird. It was full of the bubbling of the water, and the sadness and hope of the wilderness—that success is right, and that the failures give way to the successful. The miracle of living is to be alive; for all those who are living and alive are part of an unbroken chain of success, whose origin began in the primordial seas two billion years ago. Not once in all those years could life fail to give life. So the miracle of living, its hope and sadness, is to be alive.

When Teeter heard this song, and she heard every note of it, the ceremony of life surged forward. Cinclus dipped to her; she accepted him with five deep dips. All memory of the old male was gone. For she would live in the presence of Cinclus. She did not see him in his proper size, but as a much larger bird than he was. At times he would be the focus of everything and dwarf the cliff and the falls and the mountains. He was necessary to her. He brought to her the secret of the seas, the mysterious beginning of life.

Teeter was stirred by the music. She looked at the

nest on the canyon wall and wanted to see it. She flew over to it and the dark round interior reminded her of the moss on the stones in the runnel, and of the grasses in Mule Deer Meadow.

The nest needed repairs. This must be done soon, but not yet.

She came over to Cinclus at the end of his song and he dipped and spoke to her with a soft clink. They flew together over the falls and fed in the crystal water. It was an hour of splendid play. They dove and swam beneath the water, they explored the currents of the flume and the air pockets behind the dam.

Then Cinclus noticed that Teeter was aloof. Much of the time she forgot him. He took himself to the boulder that split the falls and he sang. He sang a long, long time, filling the canyon with music.

Finally Teeter stopped feeding and flew to the runnel near the dam. She pecked at the moss.

That was all she would do that day. The earth must tilt her longer into the sun, Cinclus must sing many more times to her and the nights must not be so cold before she would be ready for the full performance of the nest building rite.

So it was a glorious song that arose from the throat of Cinclus when he saw one day, soon after, the silhouette of Teeter and the blade of grass against the sky.

The song burst from the canyon like spray, so that even Canis, the coyote, stopped his hungry search of the land to listen.

Cinclus sang almost without letup for the next three days, as if he were accompanying Teeter in her arduous rhythms of flight between the canyon wall and Mule Deer Meadow.

Finally she stood in the doorway of the home and looked at Cinclus. Her eyelids flashed quickly. Softly, like the rising bubbles of a spring, then fuller and stronger until it rose above the thunder of the falling cascade, came the song of Cinclus. The nest was lined and ready.

Cinclus had never performed the last nuptial song-dance of the dipper birds, but that evening he sang as he zig-zagged between the walls of the canyon.

He looked down at Teeter, filling the doorway of the nest, and he banked and side-slipped across the canyon, climbed higher and slipped back along the limestone wall.

Now the Townsend's solitaire heard the flight-song of the ouzel, and he tilted his head that he might hear each perfect note.

Teeter did not move, nor did she take her eyes from this gleaming dancer in the sky. He spread his primary feathers like fingers pushing against the air, turned over and dropped onto the top of the nest.

Teeter could not see the immense wall of limestone. Only Cinclus and the nest were there, but she could still see the waterfall. She flew into it and let herself be dragged to the bottom by an undercurrent. Gently her toes locked in a crack between the stones and she walked into stiller water and fed avidly.

Her intense concentration on Cinclus was instantly replaced by her intense interest in food. The high emotional pitch that she had reached while lining the nest had exhausted her body and she required almost her weight in larvae.

Cinclus followed her into the flume. He would not let her forget him now. He fed beside her. They arose in a single flash from the water and flew up the stream.

The following morning Cinclus danced for her in the canyon again. Dawn was still in the peaks, coloring them orange and rose. The light in the canyon was so faint that Teeter could barely see the performer.

She felt him everywhere; and as the light increased she could see nothing but Cinclus. Now there was no wall, no canyon, no waterfall. Only Cinclus. He filled her entire world.

EGGS

THE next day a series of heavy rainstorms rumbled into Gothic. Teeter and Cinclus flew to shelter during only one of the storms. The others did not stop them because the ouzels lived continually in water. Furthermore they were busy. The singing of a song erased the rain, as did a last stalk of grass that Teeter wanted to mold into the lining of the nest.

Over the hill of bobbing avalanche lilies and down the road to Gothic, the storms were of great interest. Whispering Bill Smith watched them eat away the last remaining snow. The alpine sun glanced off the white snow and did not melt it, but the rain did.

Bill was thinking that it would not be long before the climb to the peaks.

While the storms drenched the old townsite, Doug and Bill went to shelter in the cabin and devoted their time to reading. They read everything in sight, school

books, mining papers, even the old newspapers that
were pasted to the walls.

The papers transported Doug back to 1889 and the
elaborate preparations for the Chicago Fair of 1890. A
Saturday paper in November described the wondrous
projects people were proposing; Mr. Macomber's tobog-
gan tower with toboggans reaching out to Omaha,
Kansas City, and Montreal; Mr. Baird's seven-hundred-
foot-high Ferris wheel; a gigantic windmill, and other
structures of enormous design. Doug had time to read
all this, as well as some recipes and medicine ads. The
storms continued.

Vera Falls plunged over its wall at the base of Gothic
Mountain and pounded the bed of Copper Creek.
Above the falls the talus slopes were spilling their bur-
dens of snow water. The rains from the thunderstorms
seemed to tax the rocks and soils, and the land sagged a
little under the weight.

In Virginia Basin, four miles east and a thousand feet
higher than Vera Falls, the rocky land could not absorb
so much water at once. It drained into the runnels and
creeks. First there was bubbling. Then an ominous
growling as the beds filled and overflowed and leaped
toward the glacial valley.

Still Teeter and Cinclus did not consider the storms.
The other animals did. Each afternoon as the clouds
were gathering, Odocoileus, the long-legged mule deer,
led her fawn up the meadow to the spruce grove above

Vera Falls. She nosed her fawn into the dense forest
and signaled him to lie down beneath a fallen log. Even
the heaviest of the rains did not touch them, so dense
were the needles above them and so broad the fallen
tree. Occasionally she would twitch her nose and turn
her ears, for Canis, the coyote, lived on this hill, and
it was well to keep track of him. Canis might attack
her fawn, but he was no match for her. She could
defend both of them against a coyote.

Over three months before, Canis had left the low-

lands, responding to the longer days, the first onset of spring, and had trotted through the aspen grove toward Vera Falls. The mountain coyotes that had hunted the warmer valleys during the winter, had gone off in pairs to find private sites for dens where they could rear their young.

Canis and his mate had settled on the knoll above the falls. She was a lean wiry coyote, her tawny fur swishing and parting as she jogged silently over the land. She had dug their den at the edge of the alpine meadow and whelped four fine kits. They were now a week old, fat and husky. Their parents hunted the food of the summer high country.

Mounds from the diggings of pocket gophers, a favorite food of the coyotes, were scattered over the meadow. Golden-mantled ground squirrels and chipmunks were abundant. Pikas were in the talus slopes, as were yellow-bellied marmots, who whistled from everywhere on the mountainsides.

Varying hares were not hard to find in the broad valley, and little deer mice crowded the meadows and the spruce forests.

One family of skunks, a new arrival in Gothic, were living under an old cabin, but Canis did not bother them, nor did he bother the lone badger family living high up Belleview Mountain.

He liked to hunt muskrats and red-backed voles around the beaver ponds. Sometimes he pounced upon the musky water shrews, but he dropped them for he did not like to eat them.

Just below the den, meadow voles and jumping mice ran through the grasses, and occasionally as he hunted them he would take a snap at a chickaree, if one of these little red squirrels ventured too far from a spruce or fir tree. The porcupine was safe behind his quills.

One morning Canis found a phenacomys along the edge of a high snow field. The little mouse had left its maze of burrows to harvest some sedges.

Canis had little to fear except man and dogs. The wolves and grizzly bears stayed in the rugged mountains to the north, or on the headwaters of the Rio Grande to the south. The few black bears could not catch him, and he was more than a match for the marten in the forest and the weasels in the fields.

On the day that Teeter laid her first egg, another thunderstorm formed in the mountain tops around Virginia Basin.

Canis heard the disturbance and bedded down by a mound of shrubby cinquefoil and twinberry. Here he was hidden from his prey, but could watch the landscape all around. In some directions he could see for miles.

When the rain began to splatter the meadow and

bend the bright heads of the scarlet gilia he started
back to the den. Trotting along with his nose in the
wind, he crossed the scent of Odocoileus and her fawn.
He followed their steps toward the dark spruce forest.
The storm dumped itself upon him and he put his tail
between his legs and slipped away to the nearest
entrance of his den.

This was the back door and it opened above the
ouzel nest. Canis knew the nest was there, but it was
fifty feet down the cliff. Below it the swirling flume
danced and roared. An ouzel was not even a considera-
tion, as far as Canis was concerned.

Canis lay at the entrance. Hailstones were falling
with the rain, and the air was cold. Through half-shut
eyes he watched the blue lupines and larkspurs bend
and bounce in the storm. The purple monkshood trembled under the ice pellets and wind. When the rain fell
so hard that Canis could not see even the yellow
cinquefoil before him, he closed his eyes and slept.
Even a father of four was not expected to provide food
in such weather.

Teeter pressed her first egg against the bare brood
patch on her breast. She did not move for an hour. It
was as if she were sleeping with her eyes open, so
strange was her mood.

But this egg was not to be incubated yet. After she
had rested, she slipped out of the nest and dove into
the flume. Cinclus was beneath the water, and the

sight of him feeding reminded her of the rocks and the water and the cadis fly larvae.

The rest of the morning they hunted and rested behind the cascade in the glassy air bubbles. Toward noon Cinclus encouraged her to come onto the rock that split the falls. Then he sang and danced in the canyon again, becoming larger and more important with each turn and twist.

Finally he alighted beside her and sang a few soft notes. They spread their wings and flew side by side down the canyon to Flycatcher Cliff. Under the roots of a spruce tree they stopped, dipped, and as if this were just any day of the year began to preen and oil their feathers.

The cave under the spruce was hung with tiny gray rootlets. Pushing toward their midsummer flowering were the little green shoots of the fringed parnassia and the brook saxafrage. They colored the edges of the cave. A pebbly beach led from the roots to the water. A few feet out, the stream was green. The color said it was deep and cold.

Cinclus had his back to the pool, but he could see the cool patch of green water in the back of his eye. He ran onto the water. He floated toward the pool, riding high like a cork, until his entire vision was green and he could almost taste the water life that lived in that color.

He put his head under to dive. Suddenly into the

green came black. Cinclus focused quickly and saw the protruding lip and red eye of an enormous cutthroat trout.

A loud cry of "zeet" came from the throat of the ouzel as he brought wings and feet into action. The still pool became white with bubbles, spearheaded by the open jaws of a tremendous fish.

The sun sparkled on the waves the cutthroat made as he broke the surface. Cinclus saw the water shine from the safety of the beach and he heard the snap of jaws as he sped to the back of the cave.

Cinclus was gripped with fright. A cutthroat trout of such size could swallow him. The giant trouts of the mountain streams were a real danger to the ouzel birds.

The big fish rolled back to his hideout beneath a water-soaked log and slushed the water through his gills as he watched for more prey.

The fear in Cinclus lasted only long enough to print on his memory the green pool by the cave. It was necessary to his survival that he suffer this fear-filled moment. In the pain of such an emotion he became a wiser ouzel. Cinclus had learned through similar experiences where other big trout hid. Teeter had also marked these hideouts in her memory. These things the dippers learned.

With Cutthroat Pool established in his mind, he was drawn back to his instinctive duties. He dipped to Teeter and clinked the signal "follow me." With the beat of gray wings, they went down to Copper Creek bridge.

There were more eggs to be laid. The courtship was at its peak. Cinclus had no beautiful colors to display to Teeter, no nuptial plumes or tufts to show, but he could sing and he could fly and dip and swim and dive.

In his maneuvers he broke a law of the bird world and flew past the bridge into the territory of another ouzel pair. Teeter followed. With Teeter beside him, Cinclus sang on the other dipper's territory. Hardly had he begun when the offended male appeared, diving straight toward Cinclus, crying his angry "zeet."

They fought before Teeter. Wings touched, bills clicked and the strong, fine nails tore at each other. They rose into the sky fighting. They dropped low over the water, a feather or two burst into the air.

The offended male fought the hardest. He was defending his home. But Cinclus fought brilliantly. He was defending his mate. It was over in a few seconds.

One final buffeting and flutter and Cinclus flew back to his own territory. Teeter followed him, dipping and flashing her eyelids in excitement. Cinclus fanned his short stubby tail and strutted grandly before her. His bill parted and he panted under the strain of the duel. He caught his breath and was about to bow to her, when she flew away.

Cinclus followed her back to Vera Falls. Teeter plunged into the roaring cascade and fastened herself to a crack behind the water. Cinclus found her with some difficulty.

Teeter sat silently. The duel was forgotten, but it had kept the complicated chain of hormones going in her body. The nest and its one lonely egg were calling

her. But it was not time to incubate and she stood under the waterfall waiting.

Cinclus preened his feathers endlessly. Another afternoon storm came and went, and all the other life at Vera Falls sought shelter. The ouzels did not even hear the storm behind the roaring falls.

That evening Teeter looked at Cinclus. Once more he filled her whole orb of vision. There was no cliff and no waterfall.

A second egg lay beside the first in the dawn of the next morning. That day Cinclus noticed two things that did not pertain to the immediate world of his nest and his mate.

The water in the flume was rising and growing muddy. It was becoming difficult to see the May-fly larvae in the stream.

A boy and a horse stood together under the twisted spruce across the flume and the boy with his binocular vision watched every movement that Teeter made. The boy was familiar. He had been to the falls before. He was quiet and Cinclus felt no fear of him. However, the bird was curious about him, and occasionally ran along the shore below him and cocked his head to look at the boy's wide bare face.

The storms were beginning to make the animal life restless, for so much water was not the rule in the high country. Land could slide under too much weight of water, floods could wash out dens and nests.

Finally Teeter noticed that the stream was rising. The spray from the flume was soaking into the dome of the nest, making the moss green again.

But she could not change a thing in her plans, even if she knew she faced disaster. Three more eggs had to be laid, this number was destined to be. Through a hundred thousand years the water ouzels had found this to be their successful number.

She laid another egg and then another and finally, a fifth; each one at five o'clock in the morning when the sun was just over the peaks. The storms came each day and the water piled high in Virginia Basin.

When the fifth egg was laid, Teeter turned the clutch with her bill, opened her feathers, and pressed the hot featherless skin of her brood patch against them. Her eyes became clear and bright, and she slipped into the wide-eyed stare of incubation. It was as if the feel of the five eggs against her breast held her spellbound. She was responding to thousands of years of bird lore that brought to her a knowledge more useful than thought. It was instinct, based upon success.

Down at the cabin, Whispering Bill was becoming excited. On the first clear day he would start up Rustler's Gulch.

As Doug helped his grandfather pack supplies and go over the food and equipment they were to take to the claim, he thought about the water ouzels. He had looked into the ouzel nest a few days ago, the day he had put a log across the flume and carefully crawled up it.

Doug was still eager to mine, but many events of the past week now held him to Gothic. The entire land had suddenly come into bloom. It was not the bloom of the lowlands, a season for the avalanche lily, the iris, the buttercup, the columbine, lupine, sun flowers, asters, and goldenrod. It was an upsurging of all of this at once. The days and weeks were not long enough for separate seasons: they were short, so that each subseason telescoped the others.

Doug also had found the nest of the Whiskys, and was watching the growth of their comical and rowdy twins. They were a few days out of their eggs, awkward and hungry. They were so hungry that they begged food from Doug when he shook their nest tree as he climbed it. Any quiver in their spruce and they thrust up their wobbly heads on long necks and opened their yellow edged red mouths. Doug liked them, they seemed to have inherited all of Whisky's charm and mischief.

But more fascinating than the Whiskys were the mysterious water ouzels of Vera Falls. While resting in the sun one day by the dam, Doug had seen Teeter go to the dome of moss on the canyon wall. With astonishment and joy he realized the strange nest belonged, not to a mouse, but to the water ouzels.

From that time on he came every day to Vera Falls.

He played on the rocks, built damns in the stream below and watched the birds singing and honoring their nuptial ceremonies. Occasionally one of them ran up to him to see what he was, but for the most part they ignored him. He did not press them, and finally he was no more than a deer to them. Cinclus even lost all curiosity about him.

The day Doug had struggled to the nest, he found two eggs. The birds were gone and he quickly slid back down the log, removed it and ran all the way home to tell Bill. The run did not wind him, and he was pleased. He was getting acclimated to the higher altitudes.

Upon returning to the cabin he took off his trousers and shirt, soaked by the plunging spray. It no longer occurred to him that Bill should tell him to change, and Doug had forgotten that there was once a warm voice at home that reminded him of such tasks. Like Whisky's twins, he no longer needed the shell.

Whispering Bill whistled through his teeth as he eyed the storm coming down the mountain the day the fifth egg was laid.

"Well, we won't get off this afternoon," he said to Doug. "You'd better take Lodestone out for some exercise."

Doug saddled the young pack horse, jumped onto him, and took him at a canter up through the center of town. The boy called and yipped as he passed Lee's

Tavern, and the ghosts of the long dead merrymakers echoed back.

They climbed the steep road out of the townsite. The big gelding thrust his fourteen hundred pounds forward and trotted high-headed to the crest of the hill. Doug turned him onto a trail beyond the aspen grove, and let him pick the way down the precipitous footpath to Vera Falls.

This was the type of mission the horse had been trained to fulfill. Obediently he stopped in a surefooted stance as Doug pulled him to a halt beside the flume.

The boy leaned on the saddle and studied the nest, and then the sky. The water was only a few inches from the bottom of the dome, and the storm that was headed for the valley was no April shower. He heard the ouzels calling from the waters around Mule Deer Meadow, and wondered if they, too, were concerned about their home.

The storm was coming fast. Doug turned Lodestone up the trail, and they jogged back to the barn.

It was pouring when Doug unsaddled Lodestone and bedded him down for the night. He burst into the cabin, and the sight of the beans and bread on the table reminded him that he was starved.

"That's a lot of water coming down," Bill said to Doug.

"Too much," Doug answered.

"Well, it might hold us up another day, but we'll get off ahead of schedule anyway."

But Doug was not worried about starting the trip. It was as Bill had once suspected, the boy was now involved in the world around him. A world of chickens, marmots, jays, and water ouzels.

"How high does the water rise at the old dam,

Grandpa?" Doug asked after he had plunged through a quarter of his meal.

Whispering Bill Smith put down his fork and raised a gray eyebrow suspiciously, wondering why Doug wanted to know.

"I've never seen it go over the limestone flume."

Doug sat still as he figured. The old man had given him the level on this side of the stream, not on the nest side. Finally he began to eat again. He said.

"Well, maybe it won't reach the dippers' nest."

Bill didn't smile, although he was pleased to have his curiosity satisfied. Instead he immediately projected himself into the danger that threatened the birds, and he, too, was caught up in the drama of the water ouzels.

"I hope nothing happens," he said. "It's a short season up here. Those birds would have to build a new nest mighty quick, lay new eggs, and get young off before the winter settles in. Takes 'em a couple of months and we don't have much more than that up here."

When Doug went to bed that night, he could hear Copper Creek rising. The rain was still falling. It was a deluge. Every pot in the cabin was plipping and plupping in various spots on the floor where they had been set to catch water from the leaking roof.

From time to time the boy awoke and sat up in bed

to listen. The valley was running with water. Copper Creek was boiling nearer and nearer the cabin, and Richard's Rapids was so full that Doug could not hear it fall. He thought about the little water birds and feared for their home.

THE MOUNTAIN POURS

THE water ouzel sleeps on the side of the canyon wall.

Cinclus always roosted above the dam on a crack of rock a few inches above the stream but now this roost was flooded, so the night of the big deluge he took a higher perch. He was awakened by the sound of the stream roaring at his feet.

He fluttered blindly up the wall until his toes latched in another crevice. He adjusted his feathers to shed the rain and went back to sleep. He kept waking, for he could hear the stream rising inch by inch, and he was nervous about the nest and about Teeter.

In Virginia Basin the water gathered. The rain water was running off the land, and the drainage from the swiftly melting snow fields was overloading even the highest stream beds and gulches in the mountains above.

The storm ended at midnight, but the water came on and on; through the spruce forests, over the rocks, down the creeks and runnels. It collected in a deeper and deeper flood lake in Virginia Basin. Finally it tore out the lower end of the basin and roared down the valley of the little stream that drained the Mt. Belleview watershed.

Water from Mt. Baldy and Mt. Avery joined it. By the time it reached Open Meadows there were tons and tons of it pushing downstream like a tidal wave.

It poured into Straight Edge Pool and tore out the side of the shale wall. It thundered over Bar Rapids and scooped the bar in passing. It plunged past Slate Rapids and spread wide and deep over the open meadowland. It piled up and funneled over Mule Deer Rapids. It roared into Brook Trout Pool, and only the biggest fish fought it, hiding behind a section of the cliff that had fallen into the stream. The smaller fish rode down with the current. The plunging water approached the ouzels' nest at Vera Falls.

Teeter awoke in the middle of the night to turn the eggs. She clinked softly to herself. A foreign sound was pounding in her cars, but she did not let it in until each egg was carefully rolled. Then the sound came to her brain, and she was frightened.

She stood up, close to the explosive threshold of

fear. She must act to save her life. Water splashed just
below her nest, and the growing sound was more
water.

"Chink, chink," Cinclus warned her. His voice
came from above. This was wrong, he always slept
below her. She was terrified. She wanted to burst from
the nest, but was unable to. The eggs touching her
breast held her with a force too strong and deep-rooted
to break.

But water ouzels had always managed to survive.
The chain of life that led back to the ancient seas never
had been broken, because in an emergency they could
learn and transcend their instincts.

Teeter looked out of the nest to see what she should
do. She saw the wall of water too late to fly above it.
She set her feathers and fell into its crest. She rode it to
the falls, giving herself time to work with the currents
that swept up to the surface.

At the falls she gained her wings and as the water
took the plunge, she flew straight out of it and crashed
into the spruce trees below. She fluttered down
through the dark limbs, breaking more feathers than
she had in the rolling flash flood.

She gripped the bark of the tree with her hooked
nails, righted herself on a limb and called to Cinclus.

Although the thunder of the stream was tremendous, Cinclus heard the high chink and burst into song.
It was a rippling, bubbling song, and singing it to

Teeter was his way of coping with his fears. He had not meant to sing, but he wanted to act; and singing was the only way he could act.

Teeter clung to the spruce limb all night. The tree leaned and bent before the water, but it was well-rooted and did not fall. The crest of the flood moved downstream. She listened until she could hear it no more. Exhausted from her fright, she closed her eyes and slept.

Up the stream from Teeter paced Canis the coyote. He had been forced out to hunt by his yelping, hungry cubs. The storm had lasted long, and it was hours past their feeding time. He had crossed the stream before the flood to dig pocket gophers in Mule Deer Meadow. He was heading back, empty-mouthed, when the flood wall exploded on Slate Rapids. Canis leaped up the hill, knocking the almost bloomless yellow head from the ragwort plants. He wurped and awoke a pine grossbeak sleeping with her fledgling in a nearby spruce. She chirped and Canis looked up at her, but she was too high.

When the crest of the flood had torn by, the coyote walked down the stream looking for a place he could cross. He must not only try to feed his family, but he must return to his mate who was guarding the pups. The night before a mountain lion had come up the creek, following the deer and the elk out of the lowlands. The big cat had found their den and had lain in wait for the coyotes. When it seemed to the cougar that his prey had scented him and would not come out, he had padded up to the den entrance and dug at it with his claws. He dug without much interest knowing the den of the coyote was deep and secure, and soon he turned away and loped silently up the side of Gothic Mountain.

Fearing that he might return, the female coyote had remained with the helpless pups while Canis hunted.

As Canis trotted along the stream he found that all of his log bridges were washed away or under water. He turned and went upstream as far as the boulders in Open Meadows. They were not to be seen. There was only one crossing left—the bridge at the other end of Gothic. It was a long trip but he could not wait for the water to recede.

As he raced down the stream valley, he passed the tree where Teeter sat. He smelled her, and saw her. She was only a leap high. He had no choice but to snap up the small bird. It was something to carry home. As he braced for the leap, his feet slipped on the limestone, as slick as ice when wet, and his hind legs were knocked out from under him by the sweeping water of the gorge.

He spread his forepaws and scraped at the rock with his claws. Dragged down toward the gorge by the current, he clawed frantically, inching his way to safety. Finally he touched the earth under the trees, got a good grip on the soft ground and pulled himself up. He shivered, then set off in haste for the bridge.

Teeter did not awaken. The coyote could so easily have taken her, for she was not right in a tree at night. The warm scent her body gave off was no hazard on a cliff wall, but low in a tree, she was easy to hunt down.

The water ouzel was forced to sleep in a location that was a mistake, the kind of mistake that the long history of the dippers would not permit. But it was a strange night and the flash flood that had put her in the tree, also saved her by almost dragging the coyote into a similar mistake. Canis did not belong in the water any more than Teeter belonged in a tree.

Teeter awoke earlier than she would have on the cliff. She wanted to leave her unfamiliar perch as soon as it was light enough to fly. A few uncomfortable minutes passed and then she could see the limestone cliff. Two wing beats carried her to it.

Immediately she flew down toward the nest. She did not think of this, she just went because she had to incubate. Her state of mind, her feathers, the rhythm of her body told her to sit tightly on her eggs. She alighted on the ledge where the nest must be and bent down to enter the door. There was no nest. She cried in alarm. Her own alarm note reminded her of the night and the leaping water. But she had not seen the nest collapse, and there was no way for her mind to grasp what had happened. Furthermore the time piece

in her body said that she must return to her eggs and
warm them. This was a much stronger message than
her memory of the flood. Again she tried to enter the
door.

Cinclus awoke and saw that the nest was gone. He
was alarmed and worried, but he had no strong incubation drive to make him see what wasn't there. Teeter
did. She kept trying to go into the missing nest.

Cinclus dipped and dipped, called his worried "zeet,
zeet," and flew to Teeter.

He saw that their work was destroyed. There was no
nest and his instinct told him that there must be one.
In a few moments he was back to late May—the time
for nest building, and he flew off to feed and sing. He
sang from the top of the falls, from the beam in the
dam, from the log below the cascade. It did no good.

Teeter would fly down to him, eat a little, then fly
back to the cliff and try to enter the little round doorway that she could see in her mind's eye until she tried
to pass through it.

Later that morning the problem was solved. Cinclus
was feeding in the little spring under the cow parsnips.
The tragedy was momentarily forgotten. It was June
and Teeter should be incubating. He called the soft
note that told her—"leave the eggs now and come eat."
Teeter came.

At the edge of the spring the hypnum moss grew in
large bunches. Teeter stopped catching insects and

looked at the moss. She pecked at it. This was the moss that the ouzel bird knew, for out of it they fashioned spray-proof domes. It stirred within her something vague yet urgent. She pecked at it again. As she did a stronger pattern of action took hold of her. She picked up a billfull of moss. Now it became clear. It was June, she must have a nest. The light and the temperature told her it was late to build a nest. Then she must build it swiftly. Something had happened and she must hurry.

Teeter picked up more wet hypnum moss and flew to the limestone wall. She recalled something of the night, for she began the new nest seven feet above the ledge where the old one had been.

THE DAWN

As he was saddling Lodestone in the predawn light, Doug thought he saw a tired coyote limp across the bridge. Grandpa had decided at one o'clock that the big storm was the clearing storm. At four o'clock he and Doug got up and prepared to go up Rustler's Gulch and take the secret trails to timberline and Whispering Bill's claim.

As he worked Doug thought how furious Whisky would be to find that his grocery store had pulled out on him. When he returned for a load of gear he slipped behind the cabin and tucked a loaf of bread in the woodpile.

He chuckled as he went back to the work. He could see Whisky scolding at the door for fifteen or twenty minutes until he was exhausted with anger. In a perfect tiff, his feathers extended, his white cap lifted, he would fly to the woodpile to shout some more. He would be in such a dither that at first he would not see the bread. When he finally calmed down enough to focus on something, he would discover the cache. His feathers would relax and he would call softly and sweetly "beeer."

Whispering Bill had already fastened the dynamite and mining tools on Lodestone, and he asked Doug to tie the sleeping bags, tent, and food on top of them. When it was all secured, and Bill had mounted, Doug looked at the load and thought it heavy for Lodestone. He did not speak about it, though. After all, Grandfather never told him what to do. He could hardly tell Grandfather.

Doug checked Lodestone's belly band, patted the equipment, and looked up the road that led past Vera Falls.

He could not forget the water ouzel. He had worked rapidly, hoping to get the expedition going so he could see whether the little dipper and her eggs had survived the storm. He had heard the flash flood as it tore under the bridge last night, and he had sat bolt upright in bed and cried, "That's it. The nest is gone. The bird, too."

Doug closed the cabin door, and checked the horse. Bill clicked his tongue and the long-anticipated expedition was under way.

Doug walked behind. For a brief moment he felt the pouting pangs of childhood as he went toward his work. He knew his mother would be hurt to see that he did not have a horse. She would see to it that he got one. He looked up toward Mt. Avery, blue and paper-like in the early morning. The pains of puppyhood stung him.

They took a slow starting pace up through the center of the abandoned town. Only a few saw them go. Marmota came around the ruins of old Jim Juddson's cabin and stood on his hind legs. Whispering Bill saw the gold belly of the marmot and looked away. He did not like being reminded of Jim at this moment.

Molly, the weasel, ran out from under the barn to hiss at the threesome as they departed. She did not linger long for she was very hungry. She was nursing four young kits and she never seemed to get enough food to satisfy herself. She would hunt with a relentless ferocity, then hurry back to the den to box and bite and play with her round yellow babies.

When Doug reached the top of the hill he was glad to be walking. Without asking permission, he turned to his grandfather and said, "I am going to Vera Falls a minute to see if the water ouzels are all right. Don't wait. I'll catch up."

He turned off the road and ran down the footpath to the water. The purple monkshood bobbed at his knees, and the big, white columbines outlined the narrow trail.

The stream was still high, although it had dropped three feet since the peak. Doug parted the scrubby

mountain willows and dashed onto the slope of the gorge.

"Oh, no!" he cried. A ground squirrel heard his voice and stood up to look at him. The little rodent held his forepaws before him like a preaching clergyman.

Doug kicked his heel at the duff, thrust his hands in his pocket and turned to go back up the trail, when he heard a mellow song.

He stepped back and saw Cinclus sitting on the big beam that jutted out from the dam.

Doug stood very still. Perhaps Teeter would fly to Cinclus. Perhaps she had survived the night, too. He waited and watched, but no other bird appeared.

Slowly he walked up the steep trail. As he passed the spring, edged with the showy cow parsnips, a flutter of wings startled him. He jumped aside.

Teeter flew up from his feet with a mouthful of moss. She paid no attention to Doug, just maneuvered her wings to get around him and sped toward the canyon wall.

Doug ran up the hill. As he burst out onto the road he was surprised by Lodestone and Whispering Bill waiting quietly for him.

"Well?" said Bill.

"The nest is gone. But the birds are all right, and there will be a new nest before we get down. She's gathering moss now."

"I'd sure like to know how she escaped the flood," Bill said. "But those are the things you always have to just wonder about."

"Bet she swam right away with it," said Doug.

"Maybe so," Bill said thoughtfully, "but that would be hard water to swim in."

"She could have gotten out at the falls," Doug suggested.

"Could have, maybe. Those are the things you never know," whispered the old prospector.

ABOVE
TIMBERLINE

LODESTONE trod soundlessly on the spruce needles as the little party climbed toward Rustler's Gulch. The horse and the man were off to work. The boy was off to an adventure with himself and the mountains.

For the first mile Doug thought about the water ouzel. A young dipper needed a long period for development. He wondered, as he listened to the creaking of the saddle leather, if Cinclus and Teeter would win the race against winter, if they could rebuild and lay more eggs in time to get strong well-schooled young into the alpine waters.

Doug did not like abrupt changes any more than Teeter did. He was still in Gothic valley, sharing the lives of the birds and animals, as he began the climb to an awesome world above the trees, where it seemed as if nothing but the wind could live.

Having worried about the ouzels, he thought about Canis, the coyote of Gothic town. What had sent him dragging home across the Copper Creek bridge at dawn?

Canis was all right. He was standing before his den, hungry and irritable. The bird that had caused him so much grief last night was flying back and forth from the cliff to the spring beneath the cow parsnips. Canis watched her with the interest a coyote has in all living things. Then he lay down and rolled the dry earth of the den into his fur. He shook, bit his left haunch, and looked down the valley.

The scent of Odocoileus drifted up to him as she grazed the low edge of the meadow on her way to bed. Canis wondered if this was the morning to take the fawn. His whole family, and he, himself, were that hungry. He could present his graceful and good mate and five pups with the most savory meal the high country offered—young mule deer. But the fawn was getting large, and was a swift runner. It would take some skilled hunting to find and drop him. Canis brooded. He might have to fight off Odocoileus. He blinked as he recalled her sharp, lethal hoofs.

The scent of the mule deer grew fainter and fainter, and as it passed away, so did the desirability of the food. Canis turned his attention to the scent of the snowshoe hare that was bedded down in the willow groves below him. He considered the possibility of taking his graceful and good mate and his five hungry pups a snowshoe hare. Perhaps he could persuade them that it was the most savory food of the high country. Canis stretched and loped off.

An hour later he came back to his den with a pocket gopher. He trotted proudly down the burrow with it, and dropped it before his family as if it were the specialty of the land. Swinging his under-fur he sauntered off in search of more food. He brought back ten deer mice and four meadow voles. The good and graceful mate and five hungry pups ate as if this were indeed the most savory of foods. Canis watched them with pride. What appetites!

Doug might have climbed all the way to the peaks with Gothic on his mind had not old Whispering Bill brought Lodestone to a sudden halt at the beaver ponds. Bill peered through the low aspen.

"What's the matter?" Doug asked anxiously.

"The old buck likes this early pasture," Bill whispered, and pointed toward a clearing.

As Doug saw the stag chewing leaves and watching them with a friendly eye, he forgot the valley and its details and looked at the green freshness of the country where he stood. Dark brown beaver ponds gleamed in the flower-filled meadows. The black-green forest rimmed them. Doug was frightened and fascinated by the darkness of it.

Whispering Bill said something to the mule deer, clicked at Lodestone and turned into a patch of brush that looked as if a mouse could not go through it. It was a dense thicket of alpine willow, even shorter than that at Gothic. A few hundred feet of altitude was measured by the plants. The higher up, the more stunted the growth. The leaves thickened and grew closer together, adjusting to the desiccating winds, the thinner air, and the earlier winter. Small ungracious blossoms clustered the limbs.

Lodestone picked a route through the willows. Doug followed close behind the horse, sensing at last the excitement of the prospector.

This must be the hidden trail to his grandfather's lode. He bravely plunged through the tangled mat and stood before the black forest. He caught his breath with a twinge of fear. But he had to go on and he walked into the catacombs of Englemann spruce, scarcely daring to breathe. He could not hear his own footsteps on the deep rug of needles. The rising sun occasionally penetrated the gloom, making bright circles on the ground, but they were more like eyes than sunlight.

When they finally left the forest, Doug began to talk and sing. They were climbing almost straight up, following the edge of a rock slide, but they were in the

sunlight, and they could see for almost a mile in a wide arc around them.

After half an hour Doug began to drop back, his breath coming hard and his knees shaking. He felt that he couldn't get enough air into his lungs. Gasping, he finally dropped down on a square boulder whose sharp edges proclaimed its youth, no more than a few hundred years old perhaps.

A marmot whistled from the slide above. Doug looked into his haughty brown face and smiled. He was about to get to his feet when his eyes met the big brown eyes of a little pika or cony. The hamster-like animal of the alpine rock slides turned from his lookout post and ran off to his den. He had been harvesting the elderberry leaves, fescue, and brome grasses of the meadows, bringing them back to the rocks to dry. They were laid like a bouquet left by a child.

Doug looked up the rock slide to see his grandfather and Lodestone nearly a quarter of a mile ahead. He was irritated that they had gone on without him, but he was determined not to show that he cared. He looked for the little pika. Presently Doug saw him, edging over the lookout rock with a flower to add to his haypile. When the pile was dry, he would store it in a granary between the stones, where the snow never fell. He would feed on his haypiles all winter as he roamed from granary to granary, burrowing under tons of snow. The water ouzel found air pockets behind a waterfall, the pika found alleys and barns for his food, and warm chambers, between the rocks under the snow. The boy thought how life found a footing in the most unlikely places.

Doug got up when he saw Grandpa and Lodestone stop and wait at the hairpin turn. By the time he had struggled up to them, he could not feel angry. The

stabs of pain in his lungs made him forget the pin prick
in his mind.

Just beyond the hairpin bend, the expedition faced a
wide ice field. Bill dismounted and took out a shovel and
pick. Carefully he began to cut steps across the ice, for
the field was steep. A horse or a man could slip and fall
on it. And once they had slipped there would be no stopping until they plunged into the beaver ponds below.

Bill worked quickly, the small shovel flashed in the
sun. Doug stood at the edge of the stream of ice and
watched. Testily he looked down the glassy slide to the
tops of the giant spruce, which from this height looked
no bigger than the tiny alpine willow.

The wind swept out of the glacial cirque to their
right. As it escaped the amphitheater-like recess, it
roared down the pass. Doug reached for a boulder to
hold himself.

When the old prospector was halfway across the
snow field, Lodestone decided it was time to follow. He
began to pick his way slowly. Only then did it occur to
Doug that it was time for him to cross.

He remembered the pick, and was pleased to find it
at the edge of the ice. As he dug it in, stepped, and dug
it in, he thought how unlike Grandpa to forget anything. He wondered if the old man had left the pick for
him. He was warmed by the kindness.

Glancing over his shoulder, he saw ice and space

below him and was grateful for the pick. Then it occurred to him that the pick might have been left because his grandfather needed some help. He hadn't asked but he rarely did.

When the idea came to him, he looked across at the old man, whacking and digging the hard ice. Doug signaled Lodestone to halt. In a burst of good fellowship, he got down on all fours, crawled past Lodestone's legs, using the pick as a hanger, and stepped over to his grandfather.

He exchanged the pick for the shovel and dug swiftly after Whispering Bill had broken the surface. Together they worked quickly and safely across the ice field to the secure rocks on the other side.

"Well, now that was a help. Thanks," Bill said, when the three of them stood on the firm trail again. Doug felt wonderfully important.

Rounding the wall of the glacial bed, the three walked into a powerful wind. It took strength to stand against it. It roared as it blew out of the cirque and flowed down the moraine.

Lodestone dropped his head, and Bill leaned with him. There was no trail here. The horse picked his way along a narrow stony ledge. They pushed forward slowly for about twenty-five feet, before the trail appeared again. They were standing on the rim of the glacial basin of Mt. Avery.

The wind was less. Doug held on to the rocks and

looked at the grim land before him. At the bottom of the glacial cut there was snow. Around their feet were the dwarf trees and plants of the true alpine meadow. The flowers were intensely brilliant above the last fortress of trees. Beside Doug stood a spruce tree. It was more a beaten-down twisted mat than a tree, though it might have been seventy-five years old. The biting cold winds cut it down to the snow level in winter so that in all its long life it had not grown more than one foot high. Its stunted limbs twisted in the direction of the winds, and it reached low over the ground in the lee of a protecting ledge.

Lodestone began to climb with spirit. He scrambled to a cliff, which was reddened with the presence of iron ore, and trotted around it to another meadow. Here he stopped. Grandpa patted his neck, and trudged slowly toward them, squinting in the uncovered sun and trying to catch his breath in the rarefied air.

"There it is, boy!" Bill said with excitement. His weatherbeaten eyes were small glittering creases in his brown face.

Doug stood still and looked. A large hole, about as tall as a man and as wide as three men, was cut into one of the bare rock veins on the mountainside. To one side of it was a rock pile, the dump where Bill discarded quartz, granite, and feldspar.

Doug climbed up to the tunnel and looked into the dark shaft. It did not glitter. It was dark, like any other

hole in the ground. He came back silently and helped
Bill set up their tent, unroll the sleeping bags, and get
the old sheepherder's stove placed out of the wind.

It was well past noon when they sat down to brown
bread, cheese, jam, and tea. They had been climbing
for six hours and Doug was so tired that his legs shook.
He rolled onto the thin mat of dwarf willows, minia-
ture grasses, sedges, and pink rock phlox. He fell
asleep.

Whispering Bill did not sleep, he sat against a stone,
with his hat pulled over his eyes, and listened to the
unending wind. Lodestone grazed the alpine meadow.

Late in the afternoon when all of them were
refreshed, Bill took Doug into the mine and showed
him the vein of rock that they would blast in the
morning. By flashlight it did shine, but not like gold or
silver. It was black ore, and heavy.

"It's rich," Whispering Bill said, as he broke off a
piece with a pick. "There's gold in it, silver in it, some
lead and maybe a little copper." He turned it over and
over as he spoke, as if his words would bring the precious minerals flowing out of the ore into his hands.

For supper they ate beans and pemmican, dried
venison pounded into paste with fat and berries. When
his tea had cooled to the point where he could pick up
the tin cup, Doug drained it and crawled joyfully into
his sleeping bag.

He was getting warm and sleepy when a horrible

moan brought him up, shivering with fright. His grandfather reached out and patted him.

"It's just the wind," he whispered. "It doesn't like it
up here and it's trying to find its way down to Gothic."
Doug wriggled deeper into his sleeping bag.

The wind howled, the tent shook, and the rocks
rolled down the side of the mountain. Doug lay awake
listening in rigid fear.

Suddenly he was sitting bolt upright, staring into the
blue shadows of the night. His nose was cold, his chin
was icy, but he did not feel them. He was listening to a
terrible sound, and it was coming closer and closer.

It seemed as if great stones were breaking off and
plunging down the mountain. Now they seemed to be
torn from the mountain right above his head. With a
gigantic rumble they exploded and broke. He threw off
his sleeping bag and shook the old man, crying,
"Grandpa, Grandpa! Quick, let's run. The mountain's
falling!"

His grandfather sleepily lifted his head and listened.
Doug grabbed his pants and shoes and was halfway out
of the tent when the old man said slowly, "That slide's
two miles away. Go back to sleep."

Doug dropped to his knees. At first he was relieved,
then embarrassed. He half-hoped he was right. He
looked out of the tent into the shadows of the alpine
tundra. The side of the mountain was still. The peak
loomed above them, a firm pyramid in the sky.

Gradually the roar of the slide died away, until at last only a few bumps and thuds echoed around the boulders. Grandfather was right. They were in no danger.

The next morning Whispering Bill awakened Doug before sunrise. The boy stumbled from the tent and stood shivering in the freezing dawn. He felt exhausted and as mean as a weasel. He saw his grandfather busily at work, starting the fire, boiling melted snow for oatmeal and humming happily about the camp. He knew he should help, but all he was able to do was put on more clothing and thaw his hands by the sheepherder's stove. He was not a cheerful companion as he poured canned milk and sprinkled sugar on his tin of cereal.

"Good morning," he finally managed.

"Well, you sound like a rock slide yourself," Bill chided. He grinned as he pressed his lip against his hot tin cup of coffee, testing whether it would blister or just sear.

Doug was not amused. He ate without speaking, feeling less and less pleasant as the sun rose over the peaks and lit them with soft pinks and yellows. When they had eaten, Bill took the tin cups and plates to the edge of the snow field and scoured them with ice and sand. Doug watched him. So that was all there was to dishwashing. The old man tossed the utensils into the grub box and went to the mine.

Doug huddled by the stove, nursing a thumping

headache that threatened to grip his whole body.

Fifteen minutes later, old Whispering Bill appeared. He was bouncing with energy. His thin gray hair lifted with his steps. He got out the dynamite and caps and began to plan the blast.

Doug knew he should be interested. He tried to ask a question, but only tears came to his eyes with the effort. Bill looked up from his work, saw the misery in the boy's face and decided to help him. However, he couldn't resist a little fun. It was part of the miner's initiation of the novice who had not yet learned how to cope with the alpine country.

"Well, boy," he began. "Looks like you're not getting enough sleep up here. Out star gazing all night, eh? Were you listening to the pebbles roll? Well, son, beauty is beauty, but a man has to sleep in this country to work."

Doug was well aware of his terror of the night, and looked at his grandfather with anguish. If only he could have been right. He would have led them to cover in the mine, and then he would have been a hero. Suddenly he felt angry and kicked a stone in frustration.

"I wasn't scared," he said in a small voice that almost broke, and the memory of his mother's warm house and kind presence came to him. It would have been so easy to work in the store. He wanted to be home, his head hurt, his bones ached. He had failed to stand up to the test, and he wished himself away.

The old man had had his game and as he went back to his dynamite and caps he said, "Well, son, I jumped out of my tent and stabbed at grizzly bears the first night I slept in the high country. Half froze to death I was, out of my sleeping bag so much. Wasn't even a rock slide; just wind. I had to spend most of the next day patching up the holes I'd jabbed in the tent.

"I'll tell you what. I wasn't planning to do much but blast the ore today, and I can do that alone. Why don't you crawl into that tent and go back to sleep. You're pretty game to even get up."

Doug smiled for the first time that morning. He appreciated Bill's story and because he did he could almost laugh at himself. Laughing tears unexpectedly poured from his eyes. Without another word, he fell on his sleeping bag and did not move until a muffled boom and a tremble in the earth awoke him about noon.

He sat up. His headache was gone and his body was refreshed. Before the sound of the blast had died away, Bill's head was in the tent and he was shouting victoriously, "Doug, boy! Doug, boy! Get up! Come see what we've hit."

They ran to the tunnel. Doug was about to rush in when Bill grabbed his coat.

"Wait. Wait until the smoke clears or you'll have another headache."

Doug sat down. The old prospector paced restlessly while they watched the smoke of rock dust and T.N.T. curl out of the mine. It went so slowly. Finally it cleared and they stepped carefully into the tunnel and picked their way back to the vein the old man had opened. Bill lifted a chunk of ore and walked back with it to the light. He turned it over slowly in his hand and his face crinkled with joy.

"It's purty rich," he said. "We'll take a load down and have it assayed."

Doug was amazed that it had to be assayed. He had thought that his grandfather was digging for pure silver and gold and certainly would recognize it when he saw it.

All at once the tremendous effort seemed silly and futile. He was exasperated. The old man had come all the way up here to get a few rocks to find out if he had a rich lode. Doug had been led to believe by all the excitement and talk that this mine was the secret of Avery—the pot of gold in the hills.

"Before we go down," Bill said with the same enthusiasm, "we'll have to get to timber and cut some logs to hold up this part of the roof. Go get Lodestone and we'll do that after lunch."

About one thirty the three lonely figures wound down the side of the mountain and disappeared into the spruce forests. They felled several sturdy Engelmann spruce. Doug chopped and trimmed all afternoon, but only one log was ready to be hauled back to the tunnel when Bill decided to stop work for the day.

After supper, Doug left the camp site and wandered over the rocks to the edge of the snow field. He bent down, for there, its roots grasping the cold snow, was a flower. The blossom was larger than the stem and leaves that bore it, and its yellow color was the most brilliant Doug had ever seen. The small plant was necessarily dwarfed here above timberline. It must escape the fierce winds and come to maturity early. Doug sat down beside it and looked at its leaves. They were thick and tough like the leaves of a desert plant. As he looked at the primrose again it reminded him of some of the blossoms he had seen one time in the Black Canyon of the Gunnison. He wondered if the desert and the mountain top could have something in common. No water? But it rained up here. He looked at his cracking hands and licked his bleeding lips. They dried before his tongue had finished the sweep. The wind took all the water. That was it.

A movement on the snow field caught Doug's eye and he looked up to see a short-legged, grayish animal trudging across the bright snow as she headed down the meadow.

It was a badger returning with a pika to her den. She wore a tawny stripe down the center of her head and a black spot behind each white cheek. She was tremendous and powerful-looking.

Doug watched the badger with pleasure, and felt a little more at home in the presence of this animal, so relaxed and at ease in the solitary mountain tops. Doug returned to camp and slept well that night.

The following day, the man and the boy got the first beam into the mine and then rested. Bill's real belief in their work carried the boy along, until once more he felt the excitement of the summer. In the afternoon they went back for another log. They worked on the mine timbers for three more days.

On the dawn of the seventh day they loaded two bags of ore.

"I'm taking a lot of this ore down," Bill confided. "I haven't been kicking around these mountains for nothing. This is good. Might be worth two hundred dollars a ton."

"Two hundred dollars a ton!" Doug repeated. Was this the fortune they had come to find? Was his grandfather crazy from the altitude, or was he telling him a prospector's yarn so that he would not run through the streets of Crested Butte shouting "silver."

Two hundred dollars meant that they were taking back little more than twenty dollars' worth of ore in the two one-hundred-pound sacks.

Whispering Bill eyed his companion and saw that he was disappointed. He poked him.

"You thought it was all play, didn't you? No sir, this is dog hard work, and a crazy way to earn a living. But look what you get. What other job takes you into the mighty heart of the mountains? What else can you do and watch badgers, and flowers that bloom in the ice?"

Whispering Bill chuckled and the sunlight shone from every furrow of his face.

The next day Doug was helping Bill break camp and tie the ore on Lodestone, before he was aware that they were working like a team. They packed some of the camping equipment but left most of the things behind for the next trip. Bill stowed the utensils that they needed at the cabin in a rucksack and handed it to Doug.

The boy was about to tie it on the horse when he realized that he was to carry it down himself. It was heavy, but he got it on his back and accepted his load. Bill led the way and they started down the mountain. Grandpa walked, too.

When they reached the beaver ponds, Doug paused. The green world was so restful to his burned eyes, and the silence of the meadow was so silent after the constant roar of the wind and rumble of the rocks above timberline.

He stood and sighed in the greenness. He had adjusted to the peaks the second day he was in them and had forgotten how noisy they were. Now the beaver ponds seemed like home, and the thought of the old cabin was glorious. The pack lightened and Doug went down the trail with a lilting step. Bill and Lodestone had trouble keeping the pace he set.

A beaver saw them coming and slapped her rough tail as she dove into the pond. Two others answered her from the opposite end of the pond. Doug saw them and stopped.

In this back country the beavers were not wary and the old female surfaced and swam toward Doug. She

was heavy but she carried her forty pounds gracefully. She focused her small brown eyes on the boy as she swam. Then with no further sign of alarm she turned toward an aspen sapling floating at the edge of the pond. Lifting the green branch in her paws she ate it like an ear of corn. Doug could see the downed aspens on the hill above the pond and the skid trails the beavers had made, as they dragged them to the water.

He moved closer and the old beaver moved back into deeper water. As Doug reached the edge of the pond, she gave her warning slap and disappeared. He waited but he did not see her again. However, behind a log on the far side of the pond there was a ripple of water. The old beaver was finishing her meal out of sight.

Doug headed down toward Gothic. He hesitated at the trail to Vera Falls. No, he would not look until tomorrow.

OUT OF THE EGG

THE morning after he returned from the mountain, Whispering Bill Smith packed up his ore samples, mounted Lodestone, and rode down to the post office in Crested Butte to mail his prize rocks to the assay house in Pueblo. The old man did not suggest that Doug accompany him, and the boy did not ask. Although it would have been a chance to see his mother, he did not speak out for there were things at Vera Falls that held his interest. Whisky . . . and Molly, the weasel, who had brought her fuzzy little kits to the woodpile last night. These were on his mind.

Although it would be good to go home, Doug was satisfied to stay when he remembered that his mother would probably plan the day for him. That would be as unpleasant as getting that pulltoy when he was ten! He was a man with a trade now.

Bill did not return that night. Doug fixed his own

supper, ate it, and went to bed. His thoughts were torn between the pleasure of seeing Teeter incubating her new clutch of eggs high on the canyon wall, and the disturbing thought that something had happened to Grandpa.

The following day he made breakfast for himself. He was doing the dishes, and growing more concerned as the time passed, when he heard Lodestone pounding around the shed. The old man came in casually as if he had only been gone two hours. He sat down in his rocking chair and stretched. When he finally spoke his face was all smile. Something good must have come from the long trip to the post office.

"We'll know in two weeks," he began. "Then we'll dig that ore out of there and be on easy street. Man, sireee."

Two more weeks, Doug thought, but this time he knew it would be a good two weeks. Whisky's youngsters would be flying, and perhaps the young water ouzels would be hatching.

Doug stopped planning, for he realized Grandpa was talking. He was telling about the new car they would buy, the clothes and the hotel suite in Pueblo where they'd spend a few days. Doug got into the spirit of the game and suggested that they buy silver handled six shooters. Bill liked that and his dim eyes twinkled with mischief. The boy was a good one. He could spend a mythical fortune, too. Finally Doug asked,

"What did you tell your old prospecting friends last night?"

Whispering Bill began to laugh.

"You know about that, do you? Well, I'll tell you. There'll be a lot of old sourdoughs in Washington Gulch next week." His laughter was infectious. Doug laughed too, and then he said something that even surprised himself. He did not realize he had become so much a part of the mountains. He looked at Mt. Avery.

"Now, it's your turn, old Jim Juddson. Laugh! 'Cause you've got the last one."

Old Bill loved it. He roared like the wind in the cirque. This was the best of the Smiths since the turn of the century. This boy would make a man.

Cinclus and Teeter had been working hard against time and light. They had repeated the ceremony of egg laying, and at last Teeter was incubating.

For fifteen days Cinclus did not sing nearly as much. He spent the time that was once devoted to caroling sitting in the little runnel that poured off Gothic mountain. He stood on his moss-covered stone and rested in the cool shadows of the spruce trees. Sometimes he preened, sometimes he just stood still. After about twenty-five minutes, he would fly to the rock in the falls and call to Teeter.

She would come to his side without sound, and together they would slip into the clear pools and feed.

They explored the underwater canyons for exercise. Teeter stayed away about ten minutes. He never needed to tell her to return, for the eggs had great power. Teeter would be back with them before she thought about it. Sometimes Teeter would not leave the eggs. Then Cinclus would feed her at the nest.

Other lives came and went around them. The birds did not think about them. They felt the young ground squirrels, the round chubby young of the marmots, the splash of red in the meadows as the scarlet gilia bloomed in full. They knew that time was passing. The

nest could be built hurriedly, the egg laying cut short
by producing fewer eggs, but the incubation took at
least fifteen days, and nothing could make it shorter.

On July 6th, fifteen days after the last egg had been
laid, Cinclus had to call Teeter three times before she
left the nest. She fed more quickly than usual and did
not take time to exercise. She returned to the nest on
the canyon wall without delay.

Cinclus did not go to his runnel. He stood across the
stream and dipped and dipped, for Teeter was awaken-
ing within him the knowledge that the eggs were ready
to hatch. More and more he brought food to her at the
nest.

Cinclus got her to leave the eggs only two more
times that afternoon. The sun slipped behind Mt. Baldy
and the long shadows of the early twilight raced swiftly
upon Gothic town. Vera Falls fell in the shadow of
Gothic Mountain at six-thirty. Cinclus fed Teeter several times during the next hour and then flew to his
roost on the limestone wall high above the dam. He
pecked a beetle, shook his feathers and went to sleep.

Teeter was aware of the roar of the falls for the first
time in fifteen days. Her eyes were wide open, her
breast feathers were fluffed to their fullest and the temperature of her body was at its maximum. She poured
heat from her brood patch into the eggs.

An hour before sunrise Teeter awakened from her
deep sleep. She focused her eyes on the moonlit spruce

across the flume. She turned the eggs. They had grown lighter during the fifteen days. Not much, but a bird, who was concerned entirely with the destiny of three eggs, knew. The water in them had evaporated a little.

The first egg cracked. It was an exciting sound. It was followed by a stillness within the egg as the tiny dipper suffered its first gasp of air. It was the sound of the unhatched baby rubbing its wobbly head back and forth in its case that had excited Teeter yesterday. She watched with interest.

As the tiny bird revolved, its egg tooth wore a little crescent in the shell. It weakened it until at last the case yielded and the little bird appeared.

It was dewy and cold, and it weighed less than a twenty-five-cent piece.

Teeter pecked the little thing, and dried it with her hot breast. Then she took the discarded shell in her bill. She could just see the pale thread of the stream lying between the dark rocks when she flew from the nest with the shell. She carried it beyond Mule Deer Rapids and dropped it in a willow thicket.

She chinked and Odocoileus twitched one of her big ears. The deer was standing not far from the stream by the round silver trunk of a spruce. Her growing fawn was bedded down in a shadowy copse not far away.

Teeter was back on the nest when the mule deer walked to her secret. She leaned over and licked him. The fawn unfolded his long legs and stretched.

Together they slipped out of the dark forest into the glowing meadow. They tipped off the sweet grasses with their reaching tongues.

Down the mountainside came Canis, the coyote. The wind bore his scent before him, and Odocoileus and her fawn stood still. They could see him above the scarlet gilias, carrying a pocket gopher home to his pups. Feeding them was like trying to fill a canyon with gophers. Canis was ragged and his tail full of burrs. The grand lord of the cliff top was no more than a tired father earning a hard living off the land.

Cinclus heard the coyote pups yipe and bark at the mouth of their den as Canis returned with his offering just before sunrise. Ever since the flood Cinclus had been roosting high on the canyon wall and the voices of the coyotes were familiar to him.

He looked down into the flume and saw Teeter returning to the nest. He flipped into the air and called to her from above the gorge. She winged to him and dove into the water below the dam. She ate, and then she gathered a large mouthful of caddis fly larvae and flew out of the water.

The sight of Teeter carrying food sent Cinclus hunting. He ran along the bottom of the stream, flipped his wings, and bobbed to the surface. He forgot why he had gathered the food, ate it and flew to a spike on the beam of the dam to sing.

This was a short song. When he had finished, he flew to the nest and looked in. He jarred the lining slightly as he landed, and a red mouth, rimmed with yellow, wobbled out from under Teeter's breast and cheeped at him. Cinclus looked at it curiously, and then flew away. He went up to Bar Rapids and gathered food.

He returned to the nest on the canyon wall and the yellow target with the red bull's eye raised to him. He filled it, watched it wobble back under Teeter's breast feathers. He flew downstream.

He stopped on the shore by the cave of roots at Cut-throat Pool. He knew the danger of hunting here, but a large hatch of larvae caught his attention, and a hatch of larvae was important to him now. He would stay out of the deep water.

He slipped into the water and snatched as many larvae as he could reach in the shallows. He watched the circles of sunlight on the stones. There was no shadow of old Salmo, the cutthroat trout.

Cinclus walked deeper into the water. Now he could see the old iron pipe. It teemed with aquatic life. He did not dare to go down to it, but even in the shallows near it there were hundreds of larvae. A young ouzel needed this food.

The water did not change its shadowy blue-green color as Salmo, the cutthroat, rippled his fins and drifted from his deep hiding place under the bank. He slid toward the water bird, keeping the pipe between them to hide his approach.

Cinclus had packed his bill almost back to his throat with nymphs and larvae. Well supplied with nestling food, he stepped up the slope to the beach.

Suddenly the pipe enlarged. It grew a fin. The water churned and the pebbles rolled and Cinclus plunged for the surface. Salmo streaked after him.

Cinclus saw the white teeth in that tremendous circle of red. But Cinclus was no ordinary bird. His knowledge of the physics of water was his freedom. He sped up, but to gain more speed he also spun downstream on a swift current. He felt his body lighten as the heavy surface water rolled back from his neck and shoulders. Then he was airborne.

Salmo leaped out of the water in the same spot. His mouth snapped shut, but he had missed. He arched his body. There was a heavy splash as the trout sank back into his water home.

Cinclus was flying. He rounded the bend and dropped onto the wheel in Iron Wheel Pond. Here he rested from the excitement, dipped and flew upstream to the nest.

When Cinclus arrived, Teeter left. Cinclus again looked with interest at the straggly nestling. With a quick stab he deposited a mouthful of food in the scar-

let gap. He studied the nestling a little longer, then
went over the falls to hunt with Teeter.

Late that morning there was one less egg and one
more bird. The next morning three sightless young
water ouzels rested in the dry inner nest. There had
been no fourth or fifth egg, for Teeter's second clutch
was smaller in number than her first.

Teeter and Cinclus easily met the demands of the
day-old nestlings and at noon they rested. Teeter
brooded the young. Cinclus sought his moss-covered
rock in the Gothic brooklet. He sat quietly. A small
patch of sunlight that penetrated the dense spruce
limbs, played at his feet. Occasionally he nipped at it.

High up on Gothic Mountain above the ouzel nest a
stone broke loose and rolled off the rimrock. For sev-
enty feet it bounced, rolled and spun. It came to rest
against the tough mat of alpine willow that grew at the
bottom of the slope.

The falling stone was heard by Cinclus. It did not
worry him. He simply listened to it as he did to so
many stones in this land of breaking mountains.

For countless years the rimrock had been freezing in
the cold, cracking as it thawed in the sun. It was cut
with many crevices. There was one big longitudinal
pocket that was filled with water. The early rains had
melted the snow field above, and the water had not yet
drained from the cliff. The rimrock strained under the

weight of the water, and yielded imperceptibly. Below it the dippers carried on their duties.

The morning when the nestlings were three days old, and their gray-blue quills were appearing in orderly patterns down their backs, on their sides, and on their wings, Cinclus saw a more immediate menace on the mountain.

Doug appeared at the top of the cliff with a rope. He tied one end around his waist and anchored the other to the spruce beside the coyote den. Slowly the boy edged himself over the face of the gorge, getting handholds and foot-holds in the neatly broken limestone. He descended foot by foot.

Cinclus was surprised that this little fawn of man could maneuver on a cliff. He had always been a quiet animal resting under the spruces and watching the water. He had been gentle. As Cinclus watched him climb down the cliff, he concluded that he was not so gentle and he warned Teeter of the danger.

She heard the signal but brooded close. She sat tight on her nestlings. She heard the hard leather boots scrape and dig for holds on the rocks above her.

There was a shattering scramble and the boy's legs appeared to the left above the nest. He reached down, touched the nest and seemed to be satisfied. He scrambled back up the cliff.

Teeter came to the door. Her head poked out like a curious housewife as she watched the boy scramble back up the wall. When he was near the top, she loosened her feathers and went back to the little ouzels.

Doug stretched out by the coyote den. He put his head on his hands and smiled. He knew now that it was possible to get a little water ouzel before it fledged. He would raise it and let it swim in the bathtub at home during the winter.

While waiting to hear from the assay house, it had occurred to Doug that it would be wonderful to have a baby water ouzel. Nothing seemed so much a part of the high country as the dippers. Once the idea came to him he could think of little else. During the long winter ahead, it would remind him that he had been a man and could be independent.

He saw Cinclus wing down the stream toward Flycatcher Cliff and he wondered what he would feed such a bird, now that it was possible to have one.

July in Gothic was warm during the day and cool at night. The alpine flowers flooded the meadows, all colors, all kinds. The shifting winds played over them all day as if to remind them that winter was only a few degrees away.

The meadows were busy with life. Ground squirrels brought their young into the sun to forage for their own food, and chipmunks ran up and down the rocks alternately looking for seeds and the other members of their family. The young of the wilderness were everywhere.

At this season the cattlemen brought their cattle to the high meadows to pasture, and Gothic town sounded with the stamping of hoofs and the yipes and whistles of cowboys. They camped in the old abandoned cabins of the town, and when they weren't herding the cattle in the hills, they were out hunting coyotes, or standing around their doorways swapping yarns.

Doug had been glad to see them come. The first few days they were there he had spent hours talking to them. But they were older than he, and he found less and less to say to them. The things they wanted to learn from him, Doug would not tell.

He said, with the same straight face that his grandfather wore when speaking of a rich lode, that he did not know where the coyotes denned, or the whiskyjacks nested.

Then one day he overheard three of them speaking of Whispering Bill and himself. They laughed and called them "loco old mavericks." Doug was dismayed and when he met them later he came to the defense of his brand. He bragged of his treasures in the mountains, and told them that eight bags of ore was all he and his grandfather needed to live for a year.

When Doug told his grandfather what he had said, the old man sent his chair rocking in joy. Eight bags of ore—he knew the boy had the makings of a good prospector.

It was the middle of July. The assay house had still not returned the estimate of the ore. Doug began to show concern, for after bragging to the cowboys, he had a personal interest in the findings. What was more, he was curious.

"Let's go mine it, anyway," he suggested one evening as the man and the boy sat on the step of the cabin and looked at Avery. Then he added softly:

"The winds are probably shouting to us up there, and the stove is getting rusty." The memory of the trip seemed pleasant and wonderful. He had a longing to see again the land above the timberline.

"You know, Grandpa," he said, "it's not the gold or the silver; it's the big, silent old mountains that get you."

"Now, you understand me," Bill said quietly. "I'm caught by those mountains and I'll never get away. All other trades seem dull and tiresome compared to prospecting.

"I'm not rich. Matter of fact, most of the money from that claim I sold four years ago is gone, but I just can't leave this place. I'll just sell another claim and go on prospecting. Some day maybe my turn will come to find a rich strike. The old Silvanite mine up Copper Creek ran two thousand ounces of silver to the ton. There's wealth all around us; but, best of all, there are the mountains."

"Beeerr," a voice called from the spruce grove. Whisky was sitting, cocky and erect, on a low branch. As Doug looked at the bird, he remembered that the sourdough pancakes were gone, but there was some left-over trout. He went to get it and Whisky came excitedly to the woodpile. He jumped onto Doug's hand as he stepped out the door. Bill looked at the bird.

"Whisky's gonna get it one of these days," he said.

"Why? What do you mean?"

"Oh, all the critters that come to depend on man, better watch out. It hain't good for them. Cooked fish; that's no food for a decent bird. All that crazy Whisky eats is what we give him. He needs some bird sense if he is going to last through the winter, and the kind of bird sense that tells him to go eat some berries and worms and good natural foods. The cold is gonna come and he'll shiver with skimpy old pancake fat. He's getting too logy to rustle up his own grub."

Doug was dismayed. It had never occurred to him that he was doing anything but being kind to the bird. He watched Whisky carry a piece of the fish back to his nestlings and wished that he could take it away from him. Yes, Whisky needed to go off on his own and become a man—even, he thought in amazement, as I have.

"What Whisky needs is a grandpa," Doug said. The old man scratched his sunburned head and tried to make sense out of that. When it came to him he smiled.

"Well, maybe," he added, "but animals are animals and people are people."

Whisky was back within five minutes for more

food. Doug looked at him helplessly and went into the cabin for the rest of the trout. He spoke to him gently as he ate.

"You're the nicest, most foolish jay in the world." He turned swiftly to Bill.

"But I'm only trying to help him." He stopped in surprise and added slowly. "That's what Mother always says to me. It's funny, but up here alone like this people and birds and animals get all mixed up together, and it's hard to tell where they end and we begin."

Whispering Bill just nodded and looked at his dusty boots.

Whisky carried the fish back to his fledglings and stuffed their open mouths. Bill had hit upon part of the truth, for Whiskey was not well. However, it was not the food that was causing him to lose weight ever so slowly. Malaria had gotten a good start in his bloodstream. The pancakes and bread did not make him ill. It was the bite of a mosquito carrying the disease. The old jay was active and spry in spite of the infection, but the parasites were there and they could be deadly if Whisky were weakened. It would be wise for Whisky not to get too wet or cold or frightened or tired.

Before going to bed, Doug noticed that the snow field on Gothic was smaller.

Rivulets of water seeped away from the glacier and bubbled into the crevice of the rimrock. Relentless pressure over the years had weakened a fifty-foot section of the rim. Last winter the expanding ice had shot a crack through the rimrock to the outside wall. Held by its own weight, the giant block rested in place.

Below the bulging wall of the mountain lay the den of Canis. The old coyote had retired to his lair early this morning for the cattlemen were all over the hills, riding their horses and occasionally shooting into the brush.

Canis was uneasy. He sensed that they were hunting him and his Gothic clan. It was time to teach the pups the meaning of a man with a gun. He pushed down the tunnel to the living chamber.

One little female pup was stretched out on the cool earth. As soon as the sun rose, she had stopped playing outside to escape the millions of sun flies that were now pestering the coyotes and deer and squirrels and men. The flies spent the night on the under sides of plant leaves. When the sun came out they swarmed by the hundreds to bite anything that walked.

Canis saw his daughter sleeping and forgot his important mission. He yawned and stretched out beside her. He remembered that he was going to hold school when he felt the vibrations of Cowboy Pete's horse galloping up the talus slope. He would do this when he awoke.

The sun flies that the coyotes found a pest were a boon to Cinclus and Teeter. There were so many and they were so easy to catch. They stuffed the three little nestlings without going far from Vera Falls.

The little water ouzels grew more slowly than many young birds and stayed in the nest much longer. They would be able to fly before they left their nest. Then they could get from the cliff, across the flume, to the bank of the stream. Twenty-four days were usually spent in the nest before they would leave. The sun flies were indeed a welcome sight to the parents, for already some of the water insects had hatched and taken to the air. The season was getting along. It would be August when the young fledged.

Two of the nestlings were males, the third was Tippit, a female. She had hatched last, but she was wiry and vigorous. She got to the doorway past her struggling brothers, and her opened mouth was stuffed for fifteen minutes before she felt satisfied and sleepy. She doubled her weight that day and settled down to a regular feeding routine with her brothers.

White Eye would hang out the doorway until he was full, then Diver would push him away and take his place. Tippit would shove Diver into the back of the nest when he was sleepy and she would beg at the door.

All day they revolved around the nest. If their parents were gone too long and they all got hungry, there was bedlam in the doorway when Teeter or Cinclus returned. The longest neck usually won. Then the nestling at the doorway would turn its back to the parent and drop a fecal sac, the excreta of the bird that is held in a fine mucus membrane. Teeter or Cinclus would carry it away from the nest. When the birds evolved this tidy system is another mystery that is locked in their ancient and unwritten history. It helped them to protect their young and keep the nest clean, and so it continued. The young of the water ouzels were protected by so many things, their nest, their

cliff, their long stay in the nest. It was not likely that excreta at the site would mean much danger, and yet the parents removed it. The tradition was established and Teeter and Cinclus were tied to their ancestors through their instincts. They took each fecal sac and dropped it away from the nest, usually in the stream. Often they would seem to wash their bills in the water afterward.

After five days of feeding, the little dippers were about seven times their hatching size. Over their backs were soft lines of fine feathers. Blue quills protruded from their wings and tails. The quills were sealed. It would be another few days before they began to break at the tips and release the feathers to cover the bare skin.

On Tippit's sixth day she was first at the doorway. As she waited with mouth ajar, her entire head seemed to light up. She shook it, and found she could move the muscles of her eyelids. She gobbled her tremendous meal looking at Cinclus. What she saw, the position of his eyes, the way his beak fitted to his head, the size and tilt of his nostrils was completely absorbed by her. This was her father. And she would never forget the image of him that was imprinted on her mind at that moment.

When her mother came in with food a few minutes later, she looked at her. This was a different combination of detail of bill, eye, head shape—all the things that make one individual ouzel different from another—but still she was an ouzel. This was her mother, who brooded her and pecked her, and was her warmth and comfort.

By ten o'clock that morning, all the nestlings had been fully fed and were resting quietly. Teeter and Cinclus went over the falls to play in the spray. Canis, dozing at his den entrance above them, heard them clink as they dove and swam. Then he got up, for he thought he smelled a skunk. He went down the hill a few paces, sniffing, and came back to flop disgustedly on the ground. He had been fooled again by the odor of the blue flowers of the Jacob's ladder that bloomed in profusion in the rocky gulch below the den. He was annoyed that a plant could so tax his sense of smell. His daughter pup came out of the tunnel, her nose twitching. Canis waited with some pleasure for her to track the scent to the plant. She sniffed it again, knew what it was, then dropped beside him and went to sleep. The old dog coyote of Dipper Hill closed his eyes as if in a huff.

The second week after the nestlings had hatched, Cinclus was awakened one morning by the rain dripping down his back from the ledge above. He shook himself and called to Teeter to begin the day.

Teeter had spent the night with the nestlings, brooding them through the cold hours before dawn. She thrust her head out the door and saw the wet gray clouds sweeping the top of Gothic Mountain. The light rain was like cascade spray to the dippers and they flew into it. They sent the raindrops off their wings with pumping flicks.

Teeter plunged into the water just above the falls. A fish might have been swept over the falls at the point where she entered the water. It would seem that nothing could withstand the powerful pull of the stream at the brink of the cataract, but Teeter knew how to make use of the pull and she hunted the edge of the precipice as a robin hunts a lawn.

She surfaced near the shore and walked along in the shallows, snapping the flies and larvae in the pot holes, drilled by the water-spun stones.

The rain fell all morning. It seeped into the crevice of the rimrock, and Canis resting in his den, felt a tremble in the earth. It lasted for only one second but he was disturbed. The earth was his security. It must not tremble.

When it stopped, he did not go to sleep again, but lay with his eyes open, his forehead wrinkled.

The broken section of the rimrock had slipped another inch under the added weight of this rain water. The whole mountain received the force of the movement. The ground squirrels as far away as Lee's Tavern came out of their burrows to see what had disturbed them. Only soft low clouds blew by.

Teeter did not hear the slip in the mountain, for she

was in the air, flying back to the nestlings with food. However, Cinclus who was gathering May flies in Iron Wheel Pool, not only felt it but heard it.

He was so terrified he dropped his food, swooped to the surface with a "zeet, zeet." The water carried the sound more clearly than the air, and the water ouzel of Copper Creek was the first to have any inkling of the impending disaster. He knew he had heard the mountain move. He knew much about the mountains; he often heard them crack and shift while he hunted under water. He knew the sound of rocks rolling on rocks, wearing slowly away, returning to the sea. But this sound was not a rock breaking, a stone grinding. This was big.

He ran along the shore dipping and dipping. His wings fluttered and dragged. Cinclus was excited.

Teeter, coming peacefully toward him through the air, became alarmed when she saw him. She looked for a cutthroat trout, a mink, a turtle. She zeeted because he zeeted, but she saw nothing to frighten her and gradually lost interest and alighted to gather food.

Cinclus waded into the water, put his head under and listened. There was only the clink of the rolling stones and the swish of the shifting sand grains. He was calmer when he surfaced.

The next five days were sunny and full of flies. The mountain relaxed, and Cinclus ceased to listen for the voice of the earth as he hunted the bottom of his

stream. The life growing in the moss nest was too immediate.

The ceremony of feeding the young was a lovely sight. For about an hour Teeter and Cinclus did nothing but fly off for food, return and stuff the yellow edged targets. When the mouths closed and the sleepy heads went down, it was the signal for the two parent ouzels to go over the falls and feed and play. They would disappear behind the thundering sheet of water and sit in their favorite air pockets. Here they would tidy their feathers, straighten the twisted, water-bent ends of their tails and rest. Presently Cinclus would chink, and Teeter would look at him. He was still large and important in her eyes—perhaps not as large as during the breeding season—but big enough so that she responded to him and flew after him to feed. They let about half an hour pass in this pleasant way.

When they were comfortable they would fly past the nest and call to their nestlings. If a screaming head appeared at the doorway, and it always did, Teeter would fly upstream to Lincoln Sparrow Point, and Cinclus would go downstream into Saxifrage Pool.

As Teeter gathered nestling food she listened to the tiny Lincoln Sparrow chip at the whisky-jacks. He was always chipping at them, for they often came slinking through the trees and once they had robbed his nest. Teeter listened to this little worrier, and noticed a change in his frantic note. It had a slightly higher pitch than his "here come the jays" cry. Teeter checked for the sparrow hawk.

Out of the top of her eyes she saw a pair of golden eagles. She tilted her head to see them circling like black leaves high above Gothic Mountain. They were coasting on the winds that ebbed up from the peaks, looking for big things like marmots and coyotes. She went back to larvae hunting.

The nestlings kept growing. All they needed was food, care, and time. They happily popped to the door-way in their turn, going around and around, and during the first week they were bigger at each feeding. When they were hatched they weighed about as much as a twenty-five-cent piece. At the end of the first week they weighed as much as seven quarters. Now the nestlings were two weeks old and weighed as much as eight quarters. Teeter's weight was equal to about ten quarters. As the weight gain slackened, the feather growth quickened. At hatching the baby birds were protected only by a scant, wispy covering of natal down. At the end of the first week, soft quills stuck out in narrow rows on their wings, tail, back, belly, thighs, and head, but the nestlings still looked naked. At the end of the second week the growing feathers stuck out from the quills and covered the bare areas between the feather rows.

. . .

The scarlet gilias faded from the meadows, except for a few late ones still blooming in cool spots. Cinclus saw the red go from the hills, as he and Teeter worked from dawn to dusk, feeding the nestlings. During this fifteen hours of light they brought food every minute or two; rarely, they rested and stayed away as long as thirty minutes. The adults tired, but the nestlings must be fed. Already the days were an hour shorter than in June, and the nights, never warm, were getting cooler—only a few degrees above freezing.

In his eager quest for food Cinclus occasionally dipped into Cutthroat Pool. He would stab quickly and run out. Salmo would follow him. It became a game, but a deadly one for Cinclus, should he misjudge.

Cinclus found a pool rich with insect life below Salmo's haunt. He changed his hunting area, but as he passed Cutthroat Pool he would wing low over the water, and Salmo would rise and snap the air.

Tippit and White-eye and Diver filled the nest. Now, when they came to the door, they not only called for food, but they looked with interest at the world beyond them. This morning they saw Doug across the flume. He was looking at them.

Doug had spent the morning watching the ouzels. He was trying to find what they caught in the water and pools. Every time he went to a pothole where Cinclus had eaten, he could find nothing. He finally

located a fly at the edge of the water and put it in a jar.
He was planning to raise the flies so that he could feed
the little ouzel he was bound he would capture. From
time to time he looked up at the puffy nestlings. After
his first difficult descent to the nest, he had decided
that it might be easier to catch an ouzel as soon as it
left the nest and before it could fly too well. Perhaps
he could do this the first day it fledged. He watched the
nest carefully to see if any one of the little birds was
testing its wings for flight.

A shot boomed out from the top of the cliff. Doug
looked up to see Cowboy Pete riding down Dipper Hill.
The horse ran into the spruce forest as if spooked.
Cowboy Pete was pulling the reins and shouting, but
the horse plunged on.

Doug wondered if Canis had been shot. No, a dead
coyote would not frighten a horse. Something else was
on that cliff. He searched the top of the cliff for the
answer, then ran for the trees.

A big tawny cat leaped to the edge of Dipper Cliff
and caterwauled. From behind a spruce Doug saw that
his shoulder was bleeding where Cowboy Pete had
wounded him. Doug had the feeling that the big mountain lion would leap the gorge and fall upon him. The
cat was angered by his hurt. Doug turned and went up
the hill with the bounce of a snowshoe hare.

Felis, the mountain lion, spit at the dashing figure
but it was too far to leap. In the town below the cry

went up, "Cat in the mountain!" Cowboy Pete had carried the news, and it was verified by Doug as he ran down the moraine, wide-eyed and skittering pebbles under his racing feet. He shouted to the gathering cattlemen:

"I saw him. I saw him. He's up on Dipper Hill!"

There had been no report of a mountain lion in Gothic town for many years. People said that they had been wiped out. But now that the town was deserted there were not as many people to watch the mountains, and although the lions were few, they were not entirely gone.

Felis, a two-year-old, had wintered in the lowlands where the mule deer yarded. As the deer pushed higher and higher into the mountains seeking forage, the big cat had followed them. He had come up the main street of Gothic in the dark spring night. On the air was the scent of the prospector and his grandson, and as he passed the ruins of the old hotel, he veered left and went up Gothic Mountain. He had no use for man. High in the alpine forests, he hunted successfully for three or four weeks.

The day the mountain moved he was sleeping in a narrow cave. The rumble seemed to come from all around him, and he bolted out of his shelter. Sensing that Gothic Mountain was not behaving right, he bounded down the talus slope and into the forest where Odocoileus and her fawn were dozing.

He was still there when Cowboy Pete discovered him.

OVER THE FLUME

Doug was telling Bill about the lion when one of the cattlemen came riding around the horse shed.

"News from Pueblo!" he called. "Guess you're a millionaire now." He laughed, as he handed Bill an important-looking letter.

Whispering Bill took it, tucked it slowly in his belt, and thanked him. When the man saw that he was not going to read it aloud, he turned his horse into the trail and rode off. Bill was pleased to see that he was disappointed.

No sooner was he gone than Bill snatched the letter and tore it open. Before he read it, he called a loud "yahoo!" He could hear the rider rein in his horse beyond the shed. When Doug realized Grandpa was hollering to tease the horseman, he, too, shouted. Then they sat down on the steps of the cabin and studied the letter.

Early the next morning, as the cattlemen and their hands were cooking flapjacks, Bill and Doug and Lodestone started off for the peaks. The news that an exciting letter from Pueblo had come for the old prospector was common knowledge in Gothic, so it was with silence and some envy that the cattlemen watched the prospectors move slowly up through town. Lodestone was bristling with axes, picks, pans, and boxes. Not one of the cattlemen laughed, for each was remembering that there had been history made in those hills. It could happen again.

The prospectors knew full well what was going on in the men's minds. Outwardly Bill maintained an easy calm. He knew this casualness made the expedition look all the more suspicious. He was thoroughly enjoying his game, and when the party was out of sight and earshot, he burst into laughter. Doug joined him and even Lodestone seemed to prance. This day was theirs.

The second trip to the mines was so easy that Doug was amazed by his memories of the mountains. The snow fields were melted now, the air was warmer, and life above timberline was entirely pleasant.

The winds still howled, but they no longer sounded like bears and mountain lions. It was only the wind carving the top of the world with infinite patience, back to the sea.

This night Doug lay awake because he wanted to. He pulled his sleeping bag out of the tent and watched the billions of big stars hanging like street lamps all over the sky. Doug fell asleep with his head in the stars and awoke with the dawn in his face.

The top of Mt. Avery was yellow-pink. The rest of the mountain was still dark. Doug saw that his grandfather was sleeping and he got up quietly to start the fire and make the coffee and sourdough pancakes. He went down the mountain for water. The marmots were waking, the little conys were already harvesting their crops.

Whispering Bill sat bolt upright in his sleeping bag. He smelled coffee and recognized the thump of sourdough batter when the soda is added. He looked at Doug and smiled.

"Well, now," he said, "who wants to go to Pueblo when Mt. Avery has service like this?"

He reached out and poured himself a cup of coffee, and drank it in the warmth of his sleeping bag. Doug was so proud he could not speak without betraying himself.

Whispering Bill and Doug worked and sang until about nine o'clock. They loaded two bags with ore and still in high spirts made the descent to Gothic in about three hours.

Slowly they walked down the one remaining street of town. Heads tilted behind windows, and men appeared at doorways to knock the mud off their boots. They tried to tell from the faces of the prospectors

whether the letter had borne good news. Whispering
Bill looked straight ahead of him, dead-panned.

Doug wasn't as skilled at this kind of acting. The
corners of his lips curled upward, but the men thought
he was trying to keep some secret. Again the cowboys
wondered. Again the prospectors won the day.

The following day Bill went to town to renew his
supplies, and to arrange for a truck to take his ore to
Pueblo.

Doug went back to Vera Falls and spent the day
with the dippers. He took his grandfather's shotgun

with him, for he remembered Felis. The morning was
hot and the sun so bright that Doug's eyes were blood-
shot. He rested in the shade of the tall spruces. He
watched the young birds carefully.

Felis was sleeping in the forest above the Dipper
Cliff.

High above Vera Falls, the rimrock had settled, and
the treacherous water was seeping out at the bottom
of the cliff. It looked harmless as it wound down
through the blue harebells and the saucy yellow blossoms of the false dandelions. A flock of pine siskins,
with their patches of bright yellow in wing and tail,
arose from a clump of paintbrushes and flew into the
harebells. They were like bobbing flashes of sunlight.

Whispering Bill did not return to the cabin that
night. Doug checked the fire, lit the kerosene lamp,
and read in bed until ten o'clock. He blew out the light
and before he fell into a deep sleep he wondered briefly
to whom Grandpa was bragging about his mine. For an
instant Doug was amused that he was so unconcerned
about being alone in Gothic. He thought perhaps that
it was because he now knew what to expect of the old
man. Then he realized that he was quite capable of
being alone. He knew what to do.

Whispering Bill did not come back the next night or
the next. July was slipping by. Whisky came to the
door every morning and Doug fed him. He needed to
talk to him.

"Hello, Whisky," he called. Doug sat down on the step with his bowl of oatmeal and Whisky sat on the spoon handle and helped himself.

"Grandpa's still in town. I don't know why, but he is."

"Gnad, gnad, chee, chee, chee, cheee, beeeeer," the bird answered.

"Whisky, I am going to tell you something. First of all get off the spoon or I'll bite your feet.

"Whisky, Grandpa has a good claim up there in Avery. The assay house said so. It isn't like the old Silvinite mine, but we could both earn a lot of money this summer, if we would just get to it.

"But the way I figure it, Whisky, we'll be lucky to clear our expenses. Grandpa is a really wonderful person, and I love him, but he's looking for a fortune, not a living. If he doesn't find that fortune then he just wants to be in the mountains with people like you and the dippers and, yes, me."

Doug stopped talking and Whisky cocked his head at him.

"Some people live like that, and some people don't," Doug said.

"I don't think I'll be a prospector, but I might be a ranger or a forester or something close to the mountains, maybe I'll even be a cattleman and come up here every summer."

The bird went on eating. Doug looked at him.

"Whisky, where is that fledgling of yours? You make him find his own food, don't you? Good wild berries and nuts and maybe a cricket or two? Well, now, you go find him and eat with him." He flipped the bird off his hand and Whisky winged into the spruces.

Later that day Whispering Bill returned to the cabin. He unloaded the supplies and sat down in his rocking chair. Doug was not surprised to learn that he had not hired a truck; but he was disappointed. There were grocery bills to pay, and Doug had hoped he could put some money away for the winter.

The old man did not seem the least bit upset by his failure. He rocked back and forth and finally said, "We'll bring down some more ore, and maybe we'll look around for old Jim Juddson's lode. Do you know he tore up all his maps before he died. He was an old bear." Bill looked at Mt. Avery, and shouted, "You're an old bear, Jim Juddson!" The door was ajar and Bill was shaking his fist at the ghost of Jim.

Doug looked up at Jim Juddson and smiled. He was a bear at that, he thought, and was pulled into the enchanted world of the prospector again. His disappointment faded as he looked at the peak where Grandpa's legendary enemy sat.

At Vera Falls the ouzel family was calling in tense excitement. Tippit had walked out of the nest. She had thrown out her wings and climbed to the top of the dome. There she looked down into the pounding flume.

Then she dipped and dipped. Across the churning gorge her father was calling to her and dipping; his eyes were flashing. He held a mass of tempting flies in his mouth. Tippit opened her mouth and screamed, but he did not come to her.

Cinclus was stirred by the sight of his first fledgling. This is what he and Teeter had been working for, but now that it had happened, they were frantic. The nest had been a safe cradle and nursery. Now Tippit had stepped into the wild, rugged canyon, and all the dangers of the high country.

Teeter came back and joined Cinclus and began crying in excitement. She became so alarmed that she swallowed the food she was holding for Tippit and fluttered into the water. She circled around and around, then ran out headlong into Cinclus.

Tippit was not ready to make the flight over the churning water. She relaxed and rested her yellow bill on her tawny breast feathers. While in the nest her breast had been gray, now it was pale yellow. Her feather color had changed; she was a fledgling. It had taken her twenty-four days in the nest to grow this plumage, longer than any other song bird her size. When she was in the nest, her gaping yellow beak, red mouth, and begging nestling call had inspired her parents to feed her. Now, her tawny breast and the fledg-

ling call were their stimuli. Cinclus flew to her and fed
her. This first feeding of his fledgling was over in a frac-
tion of a second, but it set a new pattern of behavior.
He plunged down into the pool below the falls.

Under the water, Cinclus spread his ragged tail that
had been buffeted and worn by the rocks and stones,
and snatched the larvae out of their hiding places. His
mouth was so full he couldn't close his bill. He ran
onto the shore and dipped to Tippit.

Tippit saw him pumping up and down on his slen-
der legs and she lifted her head. Her stomach was so
empty it hurt. She looked at Cinclus, then at the roaring water, and back at Cinclus.

Cinclus ran a few steps one way, turned and ran a
few steps the other way, dipped and ran again. To say
that he was nervous would not be enough. No other
animal can get quite as excited as a bird; and at fledging time they all but explode.

Tippit looked at the food, and tried her wings again.
The cries of her parents grew wilder and wilder. Tippit
was excited. She screamed and flapped her wings. She
ran around and around in a circle, and finally, as she
heard her father deeking and checking, she ran off the
top of the dome, spread her wings, and pumped them
for all her life.

Tippit was airborne. She was out above the growling cascade. She flapped, but she could not stay aloft.
Down, down, down she came.

She hit the Niobrara limestone with the soft pillow of feathers under her tail, and skidded to a halt. Tippit had made the crossing and was ready to begin her life as a water ouzel.

She opened her mouth and was stuffed with offerings from the cold glacial waters. Cinclus and Teeter went down in the stream for more and more. At last Tippit could not swallow another bit of food. Her head pulled back; she was contented and sleepy.

Cinclus gave her a signal to follow him and he ran toward the dam. The fluffy little shadow followed him. He led her to the shallow water, and without hesitating swam to the foot of the dam.

Tippit touched the water, jumped back and looked at it. The clear water surprised her, it was more resistant than the air. She thrust her head into it, felt the tightness and weight of it and instinctively bathed.

She walked down under the water and fluttered her wings. She held her breath and her nose sealed without her knowing it. She learned that this third element of the dipper was wet, and she held her feathers close. As she stood on the bottom of the stream she adjusted her eyes in order to see in this heavier, moving environment. Then she came out of the water and ran over to her father who was dipping close to the dam.

The ceremony of fledging for the young ouzel was completed. For thousands of generations every young ouzel had repeated this ritual; from the nest across the

turbulent waters to the earth; from the earth to the water. Tippit still had much to learn, but she was now initiated into the third medium of the ouzel birds—the water.

She stopped when she reached Cinclus. He indicated that she should climb the beams. She did and found a protected niche on which to stand. Then Cinclus left her, and she was alone under the falls. The spray was bright with sunlight, and she was terribly sleepy.

There was an understanding between Cinclus and Teeter. Cinclus would feed Tippit. Teeter would return with food to the two nestlings on the canyon wall.

Cinclus kept Tippit hidden under the spray. She dared not follow him on his trips. He called to her when he returned with food, and she answered with her new "chip" of the fledgling. As he fed her, her cry was again the "eeeee" of the nestling.

The tiny bird suffering her first enormous emotions of freedom was only a speck under the falling water in the canyon. The forests rose around her, the peaks rose above the forest, and the infinite sky rose up forever above the Colorado Rockies.

But she was there and this meant tremendous things. It meant that there were great mountains in the United States; that they were forested, and inhabited by the lions, the deers, the coyotes, the marmots, the

ground squirrels, the weasels; it meant that the waters were crystal clear in the canyons; and that there could be water ouzels. If any of these things changed the balance would be disturbed and there would be no dippers. The presence of the little ouzel meant that the mountain tops were as they should be. The summit of the Rockies was in good health.

In the afternoon Tippit became curious about the rocks and stones and water around her. Cinclus was quick to sense this and called to her to follow him.

She ran behind him along the shore to the head of the falls. She stopped on the highest point, looked down the cascade, then flapped and flew out over it. It rumbled and tumbled below her. She glanced down, saw a large stone in the pool at the foot of the falls and aimed for it.

Tippit landed safely and looked around for her father. He was nearby with food. She started to fly to him.

Cinclus would not permit this. There were hawks combing the waterways, looking for nestlings unable to dodge. He directed her under the big boom of Vera Falls, and fed her.

Tippit instinctively understood from her father's actions that she must remain hidden. She walked far under the falls, found a stone where nothing but minute organisms lived and pulled one leg up into her breast feathers. She tried to preen, but her beak missed the spot she sought. Not in the least dismayed she went on as if she were doing a fine job.

She heard a call note from her father, and chipped in answer. A moment later she saw Cinclus fly in under the falls. He came to her, fed her, and was off. Tippit swallowed and stopped calling. The edge of the water caught her eye. She pecked at it. A tiny crustacean crawled away. She saw it and stabbed at it. She missed, fluffed her feathers, and dozed.

THE RIMROCK

T HE morning threatened rain. Whispering Bill
decided not to attempt a climb to his mine.
Doug set out for the dipper nest. He listened
to the thunder and watched the clouds gather
behind Gothic peak. He stretched out under his spruce
and chewed the stalk of an orange paintbrush. The
alpine meadows were glowing with the pert blossoms
of these flowers.

Doug stood up and looked carefully at the dipper
nest, for he thought he saw only two nestlings. He
looked piercingly into the nest. He was right! He ran
to the edge of the falls and looked down, he ran to the
miners' dam and splashed into the water trying to flush
the young bird. He found no trace of Tippit.

The thunder grew increasingly louder, and Doug
looked at the storm above Gothic peak. It was moving
eastward, a sure sign of rain. He decided to go back to
the cabin before it poured. Then he saw Diver walk

right out of the nest to meet his mother returning with food.

Teeter knew it was going to rain and she did not try to lure Diver from the nest. This was no time to begin the ceremony of fledging. She dove into the flume about seven times and stuffed him so that he had no desire to move. He rocked sleepily on the nest.

Doug sat in a trance. This bird was to be his. The clouds were coming down the side of the mountain, but the boy did not see them any more.

Diver digested his food and awoke. He looked at the gleaming spray in the gorge. He must fly.

The storm broke upon the mountain just above the rimrock. It lashed the water across the face of Gothic, and deluged the land.

The rain poured into the fissure behind the rock, and once more the great chunk of stone sagged under the weight of the water.

Felis, the mountain lion, was holed up in an excellent den about one hundred yards to the right of the rimrock. He had dragged a young mule deer under a big boulder one night and after he had eaten his fill, he had looked for a place to cache it. Behind the boulder was a hole that led into a cave. He slipped into it and found himself in a big horizontal shaft. It was man-made.

He stirred the bats as he paced down the tunnel. The females squeaked and zoomed. When the lion entered, they hung their tiny squirming young together

in a nursery. One female remained with the young as nursemaid while the other females flew around Felis.

Some swept under the boulder where Felis had entered and darted into the light. Some came back to nurse their young.

Felis explored the tunnel, sniffed the wooden beams and returned to drag his kill farther into the shelter. This was an excellent hideout. It was well protected from the cowboys who were combing the hills for him, and was just above the meadow where the mule deer fed.

Felis, the mountain lion of Gothic Mountain, did not know that he had found old Jim Juddson's coveted lode.

The flesh wound that Felis had suffered was almost healed, but his hatred for man was raw. He knew where Doug was and he kept him in mind.

But Felis was sleeping soundly when the thunderstorm of this particular day broke over his mountain. It was a severe storm, but the cat was undisturbed. He came out of his sleep just enough to hear that it was thundering and raining. He stretched in his snug mine shaft and listened to the rain.

At Vera Falls Tippit went behind the waterfall when the storm broke. Her father joined her and they preened and fluffed and rested. Occasionally he flew out for food.

The thunder and lightning was alarming to Diver. It

was impossible for him to go back into the nest; there were no free spaces or footholds at the door.

Teeter knew that no more deeks and warnings from her could keep him from flying. This was not a good time for Diver to take this step toward adulthood, but she would do her part to help him.

Diver flew out into the rain and across the flume.

Doug came out of the spruce shelter and ran toward the excited fledgling. He held his breath and cupped his hands.

A brilliant flash of lightning was followed by an immediate explosion of thunder. Startled, the boy looked up at Gothic.

The lightning hit a tall spruce standing on the rim-rock. The whole mountain shuddered and groaned.

Doug looked in horror and fascination as he saw the side of the mountain tremble and bulge forward. The cliff bellied and seemed to hang in space; each rock in its place.

Then the mountain fell! Millions of boulders flew out into space, broke into stones and hurtled down the mountain. The noise was so loud, Doug heard it with pain; then he could not hear at all.

He was terrified. He could not run. Instead he calmly stooped down and picked up the tiny water ouzel. He came to his wits, turned and ran.

Doug climbed the trail like a deer; but he felt as if

he were all iron. Halfway up the steep trail, he again
became aware of the boom of the falling mountainside.
It seemed to press him into the ground. He gained the
road and stopped. Stones were raining all around him.
He looked up to see the sky fill with rocks. They hit
the earth and bounced like rubber balls. He had to run;
and he did.

A little huddle of men stood in the road beside Lee's
Tavern. Whispering Bill Smith was among them. He
knew Doug had gone to Vera Falls and fear for the
boy's life drained the blood from his face.

"Doug's in there!" he whispered to the men. No one
was able to move.

The rocks poured down the mountain like water.
They moaned and exploded, and rolled on and on and
on and on.

"Look!" Someone cried and pointed up the road.

The boy was running out of the mist of stone frag-
ments. He came past the old orehouse, the cattlemen's
cabin, Jim Juddson's ruins, and stumbled into the arms
of the men at Lee's Tavern.

Tears poured down Whispering Bill's leathery face.
He slipped his arms gently around the trembling boy.

The slide lasted only minutes more, and then there
was silence. A few rocks that were still not balanced,
bounced free from time to time and crashed down the
slope. A smoke of finely powdered stone descended

like a shroud over the open gash in the mountain.

It was ten minutes before anyone could take his eyes off the mountain and speak. It was Doug who broke the spell. He felt the little bird struggle in his hands, and he remembered that he had a water ouzel. He looked down at the small compact body with its dense feathers and stubby tail. Its bright eyes were clear and untroubled. He said, "I have a water ouzel."

The men began to move when Doug spoke and the frieze of human bodies came to life. They gathered around the boy. Some one said, "He does!"

"Oh, a wonderful, wonderful bird." It was Whispering Bill speaking very quietly. "He loves the most beautiful places in the world."

The man and the boy laughed. It seemed terribly funny. The cowboys laughed. They all laughed, and then they cried; and they looked back at Gothic and were frightened by the tremendous power of the earth.

They came closer to Doug and the bird. They did not ask Doug what he remembered of the experience. They concentrated on the bright little thing in his hand.

It was really not a very beautiful bird. There were many in the mountains that were more lovely, but Cowboy Pete said, "It looks like a nugget."

"Yes," said Mr. Lander, the cattle owner. "It sure does."

Not one of the hard-working men thought that it was strange to study a little bird just after the mountain had slid into the valley.

It was half an hour later when Mr. Lander said, "It's pouring rain, and we're all soaked to the skin."

THE END OF THE SLIDE

THE rockslide stopped at the top of Dipper Hill, and the falls and the stream were spared the worst of the avalanche. They did not escape entirely, for rocks were hurled over the ground for half a mile around, and the vibrations from the falling mountain were almost as mortal as the stones.

The boy ran out of the holocaust, but the birds and animals stayed. Tippit was under the waterfall. The great wall of rock that made the cascade moaned and trembled. She sat still waiting for a signal from her father. She heard nothing, so she did not move. The mountain roared, dust floated in the air, and the water turned white as boulders splashed into it. The cascade rolled on, and deflected some of the plunging rocks. Tippit froze with fear and watched the world fall apart.

Cinclus was in Iron Wheel Pool. He was listening to the water. The sound that he had so feared was beginning again. He left the pool immediately. He thought of his fledgling but the air was filled with bits of the mountains, rocks, and trees, and he dared go no closer to the falls than his Gothic brooklet. He stood still, protected by his own inability to move.

Teeter had gone to Lincoln Sparrow Point, to get food for Diver. She was far enough away from the slide to fear for her home, not herself. She dipped, then stood still and watched the avalanche creep down to her cliff. Behind her the frightened chip of the Lincoln sparrow was swallowed in the thunder of the falling mountainside.

In the nest on the cliff above the flume, White-eye, the last of the fledglings, felt the Niobrara limestone wall shake like a leaf. He flew from the nest unattended and without ceremony. He was too frightened to make the flight to the other shore and dropped into the racing gorge. Before he could paddle to land, the violent water tossed him over the falls. It soaked his feathers, and hurled him into the pool below. A wet ouzel is like any other bird. Its magic is in its feathers and toes, and White-eye had lost control of both.

When the last few stones had plunged to their resting places, Cinclus winged into the smoky air and dashed toward Vera Falls. He deeked and deeked and deeked. The Townsend solitaire was screaming his fright cry, the Lincoln sparrow his. The birds in the spruce forest were crying in alarm.

Cinclus stood on a new rock in the center of the pool and called to the waterfall. He was answered by a chip. Through the veil he could see the drooped wings flutter, and the red mouth gaping.

Cinclus plunged into the stream, glad to be out of the stone-smoke, and looked for hatching mayflies. But they had been tossed and thrown by the water, sloshing in response to the shaking mountain, and he found but a few stunned ones.

He fed Tippit what he could find and flew up the falls to the nest. The nestlings would need food, too. He ran along the edge of the stream looking for sun flies but they had burst away from the smoke and the once rich water edge was barren.

There were no calls from the nest. Cinclus flew onto the wall and thrust his head into the misshapen dome. It was empty. He looked again to make sure. No hungry birds reached out to him. He flew to the edge of the flume and called. Tippit answered from the bottom of the falls.

Teeter winged in and dropped lightly on the dam. The big beams had shifted and some were gone. She was frightened by the change. Cinclus frightened her more. He was running in and out of the dam spray calling and calling. Teeter flew to the nest and saw that it

was empty. Her voice joined in the "where are you" cry of the dipper.

They hunted and called until sundown and then sought their roosts. Cinclus went under the waterfall with Tippit. His white eyelid flicked as he picked his shoulder feathers before burying his bill in them. Teeter roosted near the nest as she had for the past week, ever since the nestlings had become too big to brood, and were feathered sufficiently to keep warm in the cold alpine night.

Through the night Cinclus sensed that something was missing from the cliff top. There was no coyote concert. The silence awoke the bird and he waited to hear some sound from the mountain. There had to be coyotes above Dipper Cliff, for they belonged, like the meadows and forests. None spoke. Canis did not howl.

But there was no longer a meadow or a forest above the cliff—just new bare rocks.

Felis, the mountain lion and guardian of Jim Juddson's lode, cried from time to time during the night. He had been above the avalanche and was unharmed; but the mountain had shaken the timbers around him, and opened his shaft to the valley. He had snarled and growled throughout the rock slide, a frightened, angry animal. Now he looked down on the desolation and caterwauled from time to time, for Felis, like the dippers and the other animals, did not like his land to change. Just before dawn he paced higher up the glacial valley to search for food. A night like this was fine for Felis. The animals and birds were homeless and disturbed. He could catch them without much stalking.

At dawn he returned to his silver lair and paced before it. He would have to become accustomed to the open, exposed cave, or seek a new one. He climbed without sound into the shaft and bedded down behind a fallen timber. A loose boulder dropped in the tunnel behind him. As it cracked open it flashed with silver. Felis raised his head and looked at it. It made him restless, falling rocks were not comforting.

For the next two days Cinclus and Teeter fed Tippit all she could hold. Her feathers were almost full length and she learned to manage her wings with skill. She not only could fly downstream, but also upstream, and she even managed to make the flight up over Vera Falls. The birds spent less time below the cascade, for the water was still murky with stone dust and silt and they could not find enough food. They hunted upstream above the avalanche.

On the third morning after the mountain fell, Doug came to Vera Falls again. He held a weak little bird in his hands. He was joyful when he saw Cinclus come over the falls and dive into the flume. He opened his hand when the parent surfaced and placed Diver on the shore.

Diver clinked weakly, but Cinclus heard the voice and ran out of the water to him. He knew Diver imme-

diately. He saw the soft tan belly, the yellow bill that
was fading with age, and the feeble dipping-dance that
asked for food.

Cinclus pecked his son to perk him up, then went
over the dam to look for insects. He came back, stuffed
Diver, pecked him and went off for more.

Teeter saw Diver from above the flume. She dropped
out of the air and fed him the insects she had gathered
for Tippit. She ran around and around him, saw that he
was dying, and plunged into the flume. She asked no
questions of herself. She only answered the inspiring
desire to feed her weak and crying fledgling.

Doug watched them all afternoon as they tried to revive little Diver. They pecked and stabbed at him, a medicine Doug did not understand. They fed the fledgling and made him run on his wobbly feet. They gave him orders that Doug did not even recognize as language.

Doug and Whispering Bill had desperately wanted to be good parents to the water ouzel, but they could not know the amount of food that he needed, nor could they understand that the rocks, the water, and the stimulation that only the parents could give, were necessary to his life.

After the avalanche, Doug and Bill had carried the water ouzel back to their cabin. All talk of mining ceased. Little was said about the mountain. All their attention was given to the bird. They talked to him, and most of their conversation was about him. They hunted flies and moths and worms for him.

Whispering Bill was thrilled to bring the little gray stranger as a guest into his cabin. He cleared the table for him and waited until Doug put him down. Then he sat down on the dynamite box, cupped his grizzly chin in his hands and watched the bird dip and fluff. Silver mining was a wonderful job. It could be postponed for an experience as rare as watching a water ouzel.

"They eat flies," Doug told the old man. "I've got to get a lot of flies."

In his concern for the dipper Doug avoided thinking of the terror of the mountain.

They went out to catch food for the ouzel. They swatted flies, ran down grasshoppers and turned stones for nymphs and worms. When night came they lit the lamps and caught the moths that were drawn to them. They worked until late into the night, for they were both too alarmed by the events of the day to be able to sleep.

Diver was not afraid of the warm hands that carried him from Vera Falls, for they were cupped like the nest and the sensation they gave him was familiar.

When he was placed on the wooden table he felt timid, and missed the gorge and the tall spruces. But he was confident that his parents would call him, and he would fly out of the wooden cave and they would

be there to feed him. He looked at the man and the boy, shook his crumpled feathers, and dipped.

Diver did not know what should happen after he left the nest. He did not know that a water ouzel did not leave the nest to go into a stone storm, a boy's hand, and a cabin at fledging time. It was all right with him that he was on a miner's table. This was his first experience with the world beyond the nest, and if this was how it was, then this was how it was. He was not so insensitive as not to know that all was not quite right; after all, he had seen his parents spend their time in the gorge and foam, but he was not afraid.

Doug offered him a fly, but the boy did not sing the song that made his mouth open and his head go back. He looked at the fly and then at the boy. Clumsy fingers pressed it between the awls of his beak. The fly squirmed and Diver swallowed it. It was a funny little bite, but it served to stimulate his appetite, and he fluttered his wings and begged for more.

The flies came one at a time, a worm was placed in his mouth. He struggled with its longness and then swallowed it. He felt better and dozed a minute. He was awakened by the old man offering him a flat pan of water. Diver looked at it, but wanted to go back to sleep. The warm hands picked him up and put him in the water. Immediately his breast feathers got wet. He tried to run out of the water, but the faster he ran the wetter he became. Once wet, he couldn't hold his feathers correctly, and soon his breast was sodden. He hopped on the edge of the pan, shook, and begged for food.

Again he got a single fly at a time. The doors would bang, the man and the boy would run out, then run in and sit down at the table with a fly, or maybe at the best, two.

They were trying hard, and by sundown Diver, although still hungry, wanted only to sleep. The lamps came on, and his strange parents chased moths. The moths were fuzzy and hard to swallow, but their big wings were filling, and he did not feel too empty when the lights went out, and the household slept.

Early the next morning Diver awoke and looked about. His plodding, hard-working parents were still asleep. He looked around for food, and finding none he flew to the bed where the old man lay. He stood on his chest and clinked and scolded.

Upstairs the boy stirred; he heard the hunger call and came down to feed the ouzel bird. Diver flew over to him and screamed aloud. Doug ran out the door and into the wet grass. He found one cold grasshopper and ran back with it. Diver was fluttering his wings on the table. He received the offering with a hungry cry and gobble. Doug saw that was not enough and ran out for more. Whispering Bill was up when he came back with the next prize from the wilderness—a horsefly from the stable.

Diver was silent for a few minutes and Doug sat down to think. There must be a better way to catch insects. Whispering Bill suggested a net made from a flour sack and a coat hanger. The boy went to work.

He was still struggling with the wire, when there came a rap on the door, and Cowboy Pete entered with a jarful of moths.

"We caught these last night," he said. "Someone said that dippers eat them."

Diver looked at the new man, and ran to take the moths that he held out to him. It was not strange to him to have a hard-riding, rough old cowhand feed him.

"Phew," said the cowhand, "that little fellow can pack away a meal. Mebee I'd better get some more." He clomped out of the door and Whispering Bill and Doug watched him go.

"He's not a bad sort," said Bill.

THE RETURN OF
THE OUZEL

Mr. Lander, the cattleman, saw Doug sitting on the boardwalk in front of the old tavern, slapping flies and putting them into a jar. He turned his palomino and trotted over to him. As he stopped he swatted a big horsefly on the animal's neck and handed it to the boy.

"How's the ouzel?" he asked, and was truly pleased to hear that he was dipping up and down on the table.

"Call on me when you get to town," he said. "I can help you make a waterfall. I used to work in a restaurant in New York and I saw how they pumped the same water around and around in a fountain. We could do the same sort of thing with a big copper tub."

"That would be great!" Doug's black eyes shone with pleasure. "Like the Chicago fair of 1890."

Mr. Lander wondered how Doug knew about that fair, but before he had time to ask, the boy had started back with his bottle of flies.

All day Diver waited for the "clink" of his parents; meanwhile he gobbled the meager offerings handed him, drank water from the dish, and flew around the cabin, from table to bed.

At noon he was too tired to fly and he sat on the table and called. He ate better in the afternoon, for Doug had finished his net and was bringing in grasshoppers and all manner of strange insects from the meadows.

The next day he cried less, for it was an effort to call. He fluffed more, however, for he got cold quickly with so little food to keep him warm. The old man spent much of his time sitting near him, and Diver would huddle close to his hands for warmth.

Doug came back later in the morning to see the quiet little bird and the anxious man. He had a netful of insects. Diver chirped and swallowed what he could, but now it was becoming difficult to eat. A fledgling needs vigor to digest his food correctly.

The boy was waiting for his grandfather to say that wild creatures that lived with man suffered for it, but he did not say it, for he wanted the bird to live, and to stay with them.

The morning of the third day, Diver did not awaken early and call for food. He was still huddled on the table when Doug came down at six. He warmed him near the stove while Bill fixed breakfast. They both knew what they should do, but they just couldn't bring themselves to do it.

After watching the little ouzel peep and fade through breakfast, it was Doug who made the decision. He would try to feed him every minute all morning, and if that failed he would take him back to the falls.

Doug stood over the tiny bird for many minutes after lunch. Whispering Bill was stroking his gray feathers. The boy picked up the bird and walked to the door.

"Where are you going?" the old man asked, although he knew the answer.

"To take Diver back to his parents if they are still alive."

"Yes, yes; I guess so, but do you think it will do any good? He kind of knows us, and he might have forgotten his parents."

"He needs the waterfall and the brook trout pool and the kind of flies that his parents find under the stones in the stream. You know that," Doug said a little impatiently.

"Yes, yes, I do." His voice was very sad. He watched the manly figure of his grandson until he was out of sight. Then the old prospector looked up at Mt. Avery and the ghost of Jim Juddson. He called to him, "Jim Juddson, you old miser you, I'll bet you never had a

water ouzel live with you, for all your silver." As he closed the door, he was sure that Jim Juddson was not laughing.

It was very late when Doug returned. Bill had a fine meal of hot stew and boiled cabbage waiting for him. The cabin seemed silent without the clinking and fluttering of the little bird. They both talked about mining.

"While you were gone," Bill said, "Mr. Lander came by. He offered to take our ore to Pueblo in his truck. We might plan on getting down a few more loads before the snow flies. Might as well pay our grocery bills."

For the next week the man and the boy went up and down the mountain, bringing the heavy bags of ore to the cabin. The cowboys of Gothic had not laughed at them since the mountain fell and the dipper came to live in Gothic town. They were almost saddened when three of them stopped by the cabin and learned that Diver had been returned to his parents, a sick little bird. It was Cowboy Pete who remarked, "There's a whole lot of things people can't do, and don't know anything about."

One of the cowboys looked up at the mountain and nodded. The other kicked the dust in the trail because he did not want any poetry that might be in him to show.

But all of the men of Gothic—the prospectors, the cowboys, the cattlemen, had felt the perfection of the wilderness in this little bird that knew how to fly into the waterfalls, and live in the cutting streams, where little else could thrive. They were on the verge of a big idea, but none was able to put it into words. But they did feel more comfortable with their own lives in the lonely bunkhouses of the range because of knowing that the water ouzels lived in the tumble of the cascades.

No one went near the slide, partly because of superstition, partly because it was loose and dangerous. Jim Juddson's secret was kept by Felis, the mountain lion, who rested his head on ore that could have built a city beneath Gothic Mountain.

THE BOY
FLEDGLING

BY evening Diver was clinking and calling. He
was warm and his legs were steadier. Wob-
bling with sleep and food, he climbed up the
beams of the dam, and hid behind the spray.

He awoke when the gorge lightened with sun. He
was hungry and cold and too tired to call for food. His
father, however, chased him from his roost, jumped on
him, pecked him, and brushed him with his wings.
Diver perked up under this treatment and opened his
mouth. His parents fed him forty times in the first
hour of daylight, and each mouthful contained some
fifty to sixty insects. It was no wonder Bill and Doug
could not keep the little fellow going. When the full
light of the warm sun fell into the canyon, Cinclus

stopped pecking the youngster and let the sun stimulate him.

Diver was sore and tired, but his parents would not
let him sleep. They would not let him stop eating
either. At times they pried his mouth open to fill it
with food. As the sun filled his feathers with heat he
began to feel stronger and he ran along the shore to
look at the water and the rocks.

After several hours he was flying up the flume over
the dam and alighting at Slate Rapids.

All this time young Tippit was feeding at the foot of
the falls with the sun shining on the droplets of water
that spilled from her wings. She found food for herself,
but she was happy to accept a handout from her father
who came down the cascade to see if she was all right.

A handsome young dipper from Judd Falls flew into
the pool below Vera Falls where Tippit was diving.

Over the waterfall, plunging like a rock, came Cinclus. He sent the young male winging back down the
stream. No other dippers, young or old, were allowed
on this territory during the nesting and fledgling time.
Tippet watched the young ouzel disappear around the
bend with her father in pursuit. He was young, as she
was. She stepped into the water and floated into a
swirling pool.

The current banged her against the far shore, and
she got her feathers wet. When she had succeeded in
drying them she went back to try again. This time she

steered with more skill and found that she could float upstream if she pressed her tail into the current, and bore down on the right side. She stepped out of the water several yards above her starting point and flew back to do it again.

Tippit's breast feathers kept tickling, and when she put her bill into them to scratch and pull, feathers came out and floated away on the water. She had pulled out so many lately. Something was happening to her.

This day in the bright sun her father paid less attention to her than he ever had before. Occasionally she
called to him as he winged above her with food, but he
rarely stopped. She did not know that she was almost
entirely stone gray, that the buffy feathers of her fledgling days were all but gone, and that her yellow bill
was turning dark. She was taking on the colors of the
mature dipper, and her parents were not inspired to
feed her any more.

Tippit accepted her independence and spent many
hours of the day by herself. She stayed near her family
however, listening for them as they fed Diver, who, for
some reason unknown to her, received much attention.

From time to time Cinclus would find Tippit and
hunt with her. At these times he would lead her to the
water-washed sides of the rocks where the caddis flies
laid their eggs, or to the rapids where the larvae clung
to the pebbles.

Tippit was not concerned that her parents no longer
saw to her feeding, for it was exciting to go down under
the stream surface in search of her own flies and crus-
taceans.

She liked the white water where the bubbles passed
her eyes like spinning wheels. Always below them was
calmer water where she could walk down the cracks of
the boulders to the floor of the stream. Life teemed in
these inaccessible places, for the trout were the only
other creatures that could go where Tippit went. She

was wary of the trout for Cinclus had taken her to Cut-throat Pool one day. She had seen what the big fish could do. Salmo had frightened her badly.

Down under the white foam between the boulders Tippit learned to catch elusive insects. It took great patience, for the insects could vanish with the twist of a current or the turn of a stone. She found that if she stood in the shadow of a rock, the insects and crus-taceans could not see her, and she could almost always spear a larvae or a tiny crayfish.

It was not long before Teeter and Cinclus relaxed their constant care of Diver. He was going to live.

In three days they had overcome his three days of starvation and retarded development. Now the adults lost interest in the young. It was the seventh day after fledging that Cinclus and Teeter fed their young for the last time. It was the end of the first week in August.

On August the twentieth, the first snow fell on Belleview Mountain. Autumn was upon the land. Already there had been one hard frost in Gothic Valley and the sneeze weeds and harebells had faded and gone to seed. The blue gentians colored the meadows. The bright green had slipped from the alpine grasses and the roadside was splotched with the umbers and tans of October in the lowlands. The sunspots and asters still bloomed—hardy little plants that could withstand sev-eral frosts.

The days were still warm but many nights were

freezing now and storms chased over the mountains. The cattlemen looked at their fattened stock and made arrangements to take them down to the railroads.

Bill and Doug made several more trips to the mine, and Mr. Lander took the ore to the smelting house in Pueblo.

One sunny August day a check came for William Smith of Gothic, Colorado. The old prospector sang about the ghost town in the sky from the time he opened the letter until he and his horse went down to Crested Butte. He paid off the grocery bill, then sat on the store steps in the lonely town and counted the profits.

One of the old residents, who had not moved away when the mines closed, saw Whispering Bill Smith and his horse, Lodestone, take the road to Gothic within an hour of their arrival. He wondered what the old prospector had found in the mountains that took him away so soon. Then he remembered it was autumn in the high country, that the aspens would be turning to sunshine yellow, and that there would be good hunting up Gothic way. Nobody who had spent his life in the Rockies would miss autumn in the high country— except those who were too old.

Doug was surprised when his grandfather returned from town so quickly. That night they each took their share of the small profits, and tied it in a sock. Then they stoked the fire, for they expected another heavy frost. The cabin was dark and cozy when Bill finally spoke what was on his mind.

"We really ought to do a little prospecting," he said to Doug. "We've worked that mine enough for the year. Maybe up Gothic Mountain, we can find some new veins. I *know* this country is still rich."

Doug was not disappointed that they weren't going to mine any more. It would be easy to make a big profit now that their bills were paid, but that wasn't how Grandfather worked. He really liked to just squeeze by, and Doug was not too sorry. The young of the high country were beginning to break away from their families and wander the hills looking for homes of their own. The marmots, the pikas, the coyotes, the deer were everywhere. They were easy to find and watch.

He looked out the smoky window and saw a band of mule deer coming down the meadow toward the valley. He would move back to Crested Butte about the time they did. He really did not want to go. Wintering in the high country would be living a man's life.

He wondered if his mother was all right. How differently he felt about her now that the summer was over. He thought of her now as a person, as well as his mother. In fact he was sure that now she would need him to make decisions and run the affairs of the family.

Doug rested his hard brown arm on the dusty windowsill and thought about the day he had seen Molly

bite her youngster and chase him into the wilderness. That had been the young weasel's signal to leave home and find a niche of his own. The young animal had actually seemed confused. It had started to come back and play with Molly, but she had nipped him again, and when Doug saw him last, he was crawling slowly up the rocks into a strange land. Doug had often wondered what had become of the young weasel. Had he been killed as he walked over foreign territory, or had he found a good area where he could become king?

He had thought then that this was the way people should do it. That one day they should turn their children out into the world and close the door on them. He thought that he would spend the winter in Gothic and close the door himself. Now, he knew that people had to do it their own way. Independence was not as clear or decisive for people as it was for the birds and animals, but it happened, and it happened when a human child could recognize his parents, not as over-whelming figures, but as persons in their own right. Going home for him was not a question of fighting or submitting: he could begin to build the relationships befitting a man.

Doug turned to Grandpa, who was rocking quietly in his chair planning for tomorrow. He was so glad that his grandfather had turned out to be a lovable old man who never got anywhere in the world.

"Let's look for silver over by Vera Falls, tomorrow, Grandpa," Doug said. "The rocks aren't right, but the young dippers will be getting ready to go out and seek their fortunes."

"That's a good idea," Bill answered with a twinkle, "and I'll take my gun. If I winter in I'll want a deer or an elk to stay me."

THE CEREMONY
OF FAREWELL

CINCLUS and Teeter awoke to feel the cold air blow down from the white peak. There was new snow on Gothic Mountain. Winter was on the peaks, and it would not be long before it moved down on Gothic town.

A young dipper flew up Vera Falls and passed Cinclus as he was preening and oiling his feathers for the morning plunge in the stream.

Cinclus let the young male alight on the water near him. Tippit and Diver were all gray now and eating on their own, and young birds from other territories could come to visit them. The more the young ones flew up and down the stream together, the sooner they would all leave. Cinclus was not a father any more, his parental duties had been done for the year, on that day two weeks ago.

Furthermore, Teeter and Cinclus were now faced with their own problems. They could not fly. Within the last two weeks both of the parent birds had lost their primary wing feathers. They could no longer get away from the trout and the weasels, the minks and the hawks. They hid under rocks and behind the falls, while the new feathers were growing to flight size. They still could swim, however, and Cinclus plunged into the icy foam of the stream and went under the water to hunt. He watched a young trout of the year make its way up the stream. It was too small to be a threat.

From root to overhanging rock Cinclus made his way past Vera Falls to Flycatcher Cliff. The flycatcher had already left the canyon and flown down the spine of the Rocky Mountains to warmer lands. Only his ragged little home remained.

Cinclus discovered that the molting period had its rewards as well as its drawbacks. He could sit under the fringes of moss along the stream and rest. Teeter and Cinclus had put in a desperate summer. They were thin and unprepared for the winter. Since he could not fly, all he had to do was hide, rest, and eat. He fattened.

This strange molt of the water ouzel also happened to certain male ducks. It was curious that the little

passerine of the alpine waters had this in common with these drakes.

Cinclus hopped down to Cutthroat Pool and watched Salmo feed. He knew he dared not go into the pool, but this quiet period of his life gave him a chance to study the habits of the big fish more carefully. It would not be a trout that would end the life of Cinclus, the water ouzel.

Falco, the sparrow hawk, saw the helpless ouzels hopping along the edge of the stream, but Cinclus and Teeter also saw him. When he came to hunt from the tall tip of the spruce tree, the two birds vanished under the waterfall and hid in their camps behind the wall of water.

Up near Lincoln Sparrow Point, Teeter sat beneath the roots of the alpine willow. Occasionally she would catch a fly, but most of the time she was watching the young dippers as they flew up and down the stream. They would skid onto the quiet pools and dive to the stream bottom, ride the currents and bob up on the water. They were perfecting their skills, for a water ouzel must know exactly what it is doing to live in the streams of the mountains. The few who misjudged were drowned.

Among the gay party of young birds were Tippit and Diver. Teeter could still pick them out of the loose flock with no trouble at all. They performed their

lessons well, but Teeter watched them only with the interest she had for any young ouzel.

The gathering of the young birds and their olympic performances were the last of the dipper ceremonies before they left the high country. It was a fine sight to witness, as one by one they flashed their wings and headed upstream. They were off to another territory to dive and swim and hunt.

Teeter continued to doze and rest under the willows. Tippit and Diver now belonged to the mountains and the waters. There was no sadness on Teeter's part, for the breeding cycle had ended and with it had died her great maternal emotions.

There would be a day when she wouldn't see them any more, nor would she want to.

She looked up to see Cinclus stepping carefully toward her, keeping the willow limbs above him. He was no longer a big bird in her eyes, but an average-sized water ouzel who occasionally dipped and fluttered his wings to her as if to remind her that, even though they were no longer parents, there was another spring ahead.

Tippit flew up the stream with the young ouzels. They followed the bright water to Rustler's Gulch. She had come to independence gracefully, and accepted it as easily as she had the other stages of development.

As she swam and floated on the currents she thought of nothing but the performance of the young birds around her.

Tippit learned much about the water and the air. She also learned about the men who came to fish for trout. One day she was with Diver and another young male. They were trying to swim underwater against a swift current. The water was bright with the fallen

aspen leaves, dashing overhead like yellow birds. A fly
lit upon the water. Tippit lunged to take it. Her wing
tangled in a thin string and she was held for a moment
against her will.

Any other bird but the water ouzel would have been
snared and drowned, but so skilled was she at manag-
ing the currents and eddies that she slipped away from
the line with ease. The texture of the fly remained in
her memory. She did not go after such food again.

Tippit was ready to go down the valley with the
young birds. The white edge was gone from her tail,
and its feathers were frayed and worn by the rocks and
water. The beaten tail looked like those of her parents.

One morning as Teeter was grooming herself, she
heard a jay call. She looked up to see a young whisky-
jack sitting on the branch of a pine tree not far from
her. It was Whisky's daughter. She had left her father
and mother and was exploring the lands beyond her
childhood territory.

Canada Jenkins, like her father, was a scrabby bird,
for in addition to the natural rumble of her feathers,
she was molting. Small white feathers were splotched
throughout her crown. She had enjoyed the easy living
at the prospector's cabin and had come to know Doug
almost as well as her father knew him. However, her
father was no longer as tolerant of her as he had been,
and they often fought over Doug's handouts. So just

yesterday she had flown away and had come to the land around Vera Falls.

Whisky had let a young male jay from Judd Falls come to the prospector's cabin. For a few days Canada Jenkins had played with him, but she grew tired of him, for he permitted her father to dominate him. If he wanted to eat and Whisky wanted to eat, the young male simply flew away.

It was as it had to be, since the young male had joined Whisky's group for the winter. Whisky would be the leader of the gang during the social season, for he was older and more familiar with the land. If Canada Jenkins had remained until spring she might have become the mate of the young male, but she had an urge to explore Gothic. She left the prospector's cabin and came to Vera Falls. In the distance she could hear the cry of strange jays. She was timid about joining them and stopped in the pine above. Tippit.

Below her was a twin berry bush. She dropped onto it and gobbled the dark red berries. Tippit had not moved since Canada Jenkins arrived, and the jay did not see her, so exactly like a stone did she appear.

Presently Tippit heard two young dippers coming down the stream. They were seeing how close to the canyon wall they could fly. Tippit lifted her wings and joined them as they came over the falls headed for Flycatcher Cliff.

Canada Jenkins sensed that the water ouzels were participating in some sort of festival and she followed them as far as Cutthroat Pool. Here they all disappeared into the rapids and Canada Jenkins was left on the shore. The dipper was not her kind of bird, she could not follow them into the sparkling rapids, nor did she want to.

She looked at the green water of Cutthroat Pool and decided to bathe.

Cinclus, standing under the bank, watched her casually. He grew more interested as he saw how wet she became. Sodden masses of feathers lumped on her breast and wings. She fluttered, dipped, and splashed, and as she did, she grew wetter and heavier. Water certainly did not improve the appearance of the Canada jay. Cinclus stepped forward, for he remembered Salmo.

Salmo was not unaware of what was happening. He was biding his time on the bottom of the pool, waiting until the bird came nearer.

Canada Jenkins walked deeper into the water and reached for a drink. A fin pulled on the water and a mouth arose before her. She was too wet to fly, she splashed and fluttered toward the beach. Salmo jumped out of the water and snapped. He gripped her tail and pulled out four feathers, but he could not pull her down into the deep water with him, and he could follow her no farther.

Screaming in terror and warning the wilderness of Salmo, Canada Jenkins managed to flutter to a dead stump and catch her breath.

She did not see the young ouzels come out of the water and fly down to Iron Wheel Pool, for her alarm had brought the jays from the spruce forest to the trees above the stream. They scolded and "beered" and looked at the new bird, sitting wet and frightened on the stub. They hung around until she was dry enough to fly and then they took Canada Jenkins into the forest with them.

A rock rolled on the slide above Dipper Cliff. It bounced and crashed onto another stone and sent it sliding. Together they pushed more and more, until the noise of the tumbling rocks caused the jays to stop screaming and listen.

The frightened little animal, who had started it all, turned back and ran from the loose slide to the aster-filled meadow. He waited in the shelter of the flowers until the noise stopped and silence once more rested on the land.

Marmota's young son was round and fat. His fur was crisp and golden, but his spirit was tender and timid. He had walked from Marmota's den for the last time this morning, and had spent many hours running from one fierce land owner to another.

He was tired and frightened when he saw the rock slide above Vera Falls. He climbed to it hurriedly. No marmots whistled from the rocks and he was sure he could spend the rest of the day here in safety. Now, the rocks had slipped and moved, and he had to retreat to the meadows.

He nibbled at the grass, then started on his way again. Perhaps higher, somewhere above the slide, he could find a home. He was climbing upward as Felis, the mountain lion, awakened by the cold air from the snow-covered peaks, stretched and looked across Gothic. Felis blinked his yellow eyes.

He had not eaten well last night, for already the mule deer were moving into the valley. He would desert his mine, perhaps tonight, and follow them down-country. A bat circled his head and he snapped at it. It reeled and swung deeper into the mine. Felis scented a young marmot on the cool air, and went back to sleep. It was daylight, and no time for even a hungry cat to hunt.

One morning in September Whispering Bill Smith and Doug stood at the top of Vera Falls. They were tired for they had been prospecting in the country around Emerald Lake. They sat down on the rocks without speaking. Bill squinted and looked at the slide that had once been such a threat to them, recalling sadly that Doug would be leaving Crested Butte in the morning.

"I ought to go up there before the snow flies," he

said. "With all that open rock I could tell in a hurry whether there is anything on Gothic or not."

"Looks pretty loose and dangerous," Doug observed.

"Yeah," replied Bill. "And I'm getting too old for that sort of thing. Guess I'll stick to Avery." He pushed himself half way to his feet and looked at the scar on the mountain.

"Huh, that's funny," he said as he sat down. "I thought I saw a beam up there, but I guess it's just a spruce tree the rocks stripped."

He thought a minute and then began to laugh.

"Now, what?" Doug inquired.

"Oh, I was just thinking, wouldn't it be funny if old Jim Juddson's lode was up on Gothic. He told everybody he met that it was on one mountain or another, but I don't recall that he ever mentioned Gothic."

Doug chuckled.

"Well, do you want to go up?"

"No," Bill answered. "It couldn't be; and if I went up there I'd have to spend the winter listening to that old ghost of Jim Juddson laughing at me."

"There goes a dipper," Doug said. "I wonder if it's the one we had."

"Does sort of look like him," said Bill.

They watched the bird hunt in the white foam of the flume.

"That's a wonderful bird," said Bill. "He'll stay with

me until the ice closes the streams, then he'll just
move far enough down the creek to find food."

There was a clinking and a decking in the air, and
four young ouzels winged through the canyon and disappeared around the bend at Flycatcher Cliff.

"That was a pretty sight," said Doug.

Cinclus, feeding in the flume, bobbed in to shore as
the young ouzels flew by. He studied them intently
and when they were gone, he dipped and dipped.

That was the last time Cinclus saw Tippit and
Diver, and he knew by the way they flew that he had
seen the final ceremony of the young. They were off to
the wintering grounds. The winging flight of farewell
was skillful. The young birds were well equipped for
the life they would lead.

Cinclus called to Teeter. She ran out from behind
the mining dam, and they lifted their wings and flew
up toward Mule Deer Rapids.

They could fly again, and now they were alone. The
day was cold and bright, and the aspens had dropped
almost all of their leaves.

Through September and October Cinclus and
Teeter played and fed in the crashing foam of Vera
Falls. The snow had reached the glacial valley and Dip-
per Hill was white.

It was late October. Smoke poured all day from the
prospector's cabin, and the elk that hung by the door
had a few of the best steaks chopped from it. The other

cabins were empty and the wind banged through their broken windows and piled leaves in their corners. Doug was gone, winter was upon the mountains.

The marmots and the golden-mantled ground squirrels were already in their winter sleep. The coyotes had moved to the valley with the deer and with the mountain lion. The jays still called, and the weasels still loped over the land, but there were not many left in

Gothic town. Even Salmo had wended his way down the slackening stream, over the falls and into the lower valley.

Snowstorms turned into blizzards and by early November Gothic was locked on the top of the Rocky Mountains.

One cold November morning when the land was in a hard freeze, the stirring song of the water ouzel belled out across the land. There was no sound of pounding water to drown the music and the song poured on and on.

But there was nothing in the land to hear it, even the jays had gone deep into the forests away from the stream beds where the cutting winds tore down from the peaks. The solitary track of the timber wolf led down into the valley.

The song came from the bridge across Copper Creek. Cinclus was moving downstream.

The voice of the water ouzel died in the wind and Gothic returned to the ice age.